SACRED BONES

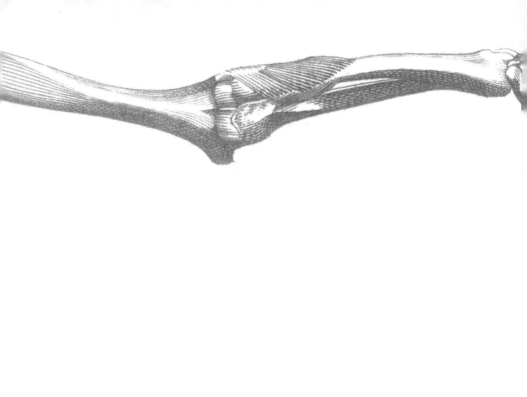

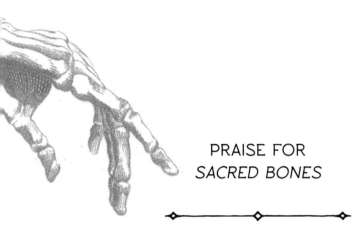

PRAISE FOR
SACRED BONES

◆———————◆———————◆

"A very warm, lively historical novel—the best ever
written on the subject of relic thieves. I look forward to
recommending it to all my colleagues and friends."

—PATRICK GEARY, professor of Western Medieval History at the
Institute for Advanced Studies in Princeton; former president of the
Medieval Academy of America, and Distinguished Professor of
Medieval History Emeritus at the University of California

"I love the crack and pop of Spring's well-turned sentences,
which make an unimaginable world vivid and compelling.
There are just so many felicities of phrase and observation.
The book is very funny, too. I was completely won over."

—JOHN LAHR, former drama critic of *The New Yorker;*
author of *Tennessee Williams: Mad Pilgrimage of the Flesh,*
a 2014 National Book Award finalist

Page 29: Random House. The right to reprint 12 lines from page 184 of *The Aeneid* by Virgil, translated by Robert Fitzgerald.
Pages 175-177: Harvard University Press. The right to reprint pages 5-7 from *The History of the Translation of the Blessed Martyrs of Christ, Marcellinus and Peter.* Published in 1926. Author Barrett Wendell. Copyright is in the public domain.
Pages 178-179: From Princeton University Press. The right to reprint 270 words from Patrick Geary's *Furta Sacra.*

Four Winds Press
San Francisco, CA
FourWindsPress.com

ISBN: 978-1-940423-10-4

Cover and interior design by Domini Dragoone
Cover art—Mural: detail of wall painting from Cubiculum 15 of the Villa of Agrippa Postumus, Boscotrecase, c. 10 BC. Praying Skeleton: "Side View of a Praying Skeleton" by William Cheselden, from *Osteographia*, 1733. Arm: Bernhard Siegfried Albinus (anatomist), Jan Wanderlaar (artist), and Andrew Bell (engraver); from *Tabulae sceleti e musculorum corporis humani*, 1777.

Distributed by Publishers Group West

To Janis, my irrepressible, irreplaceable partner and friend

and to
Evan, Declan, Josh, and Sister Sue

SACRED BONES

CONFESSIONS *of a* MEDIEVAL GRAVE ROBBER

based on a true story

MICHAEL SPRING

FOUR WINDS
— PRESS —

SAN FRANCISCO

THE KINGS & EMPERORS

~

CHARLEMAGNE (CHARLES I)

born 742, died 814

768-814 King of the Franks

800-814 Emperor of the Romans

LOUIS I (CHARLES'S SON; LOUIS THE PIOUS)

born 778, died 840

781-814 King of Aquitaine

814-840 King of the Franks

(Charlemagne oversaw Louis's coronation as co-emperor)

THE ABBOTS

~

EINHARD

(author of *The Life of Charlemagne*; private secretary to Louis I)

born 775, died 840

HILDOIN

(chaplain to Louis I; abbot of the Abbey of
Saint Médard in Soissons)

born 775, died 840

THE POPES (BISHOPS OF ROME)

~

LEO III
Dec. 795-June 816

STEPHEN IV
June 816-Jan. 817

PASCHAL I
Jan. 817-Feb. 824

EUGENIUS II
June 824-Aug. 827

VALENTINE
Aug. 827-Sept. 827

GREGORY IV
Dec. 827-Jan. 844

ONE

DEUSDONA IS THE NAME I GO BY. "GOD'S GIFT."
I'D PREFER THE NAME OF A ROMAN SENATOR:
PUBLIUS, SAY, OR MARCIUS—SOMEONE WHO
gave his life to public service back in the days of the Republic,
when Rome was the center of the world, not Aachen. But you
can't improve on Deusdona, not if you make a living buying and
selling sacred bones. It's a name that has given me instant credibility in a competitive field, and helped me grow my business.

My real name is buried with my mother, who died bringing
me into the world, and with my father, who disappeared under a
new moon in the year of the Great Flood. More than forty winters
later, I still wake in the night and see the waters bursting through
the Flaminian Gates, ripping them from their hinges, sweeping
over the walls to the foot of the Capitoline Hill. My father leans
against a toppled pillar near the Forum, enjoying the sonorities of

Virgil's *Georgics,* when suddenly the waters engulf him. He calls out a name, but all I can hear are the rushing waters.

Neighbors brought me to the orphanage at Saint Peter's, where I grew up in the company of monks and priests. They still visit me in my sleep. I see their pale, eager faces peering out at me from behind their hoods, and feel the terrible sweetness of their touch.

I longed to be educated in the Lateran with the *cubicularii,* in personal attendance on the pope, but that was a preferment reserved for the sons of the wealthy. I was sent instead to a school for priests, in the glow of Saint Peter's, outside the city walls. I was only seven, but I was sure God was banishing me for my sins. Exile could not have been a harsher punishment. Years passed before I understood that God wanted me to grow up in Peter's presence, at the spiritual heart of the Church. The Lateran occupied a green and airy site, surrounded by gardens and vineyards. It was gifted to the Church by Constantine himself. But the pope was isolated there with his scribes and legates, away from the people. When pilgrims arrived in Rome, it was Peter's bones, not the pope's, they went to see. Our current Father, Gregory, still has to cross town to celebrate High Mass. It's a wonderful procession, but each time he passes I want to shout out, "You're the Keeper of the Keys of Heaven and Hell, not just the bishop of a powerful See. Move closer to Peter's rock and leave the Lateran to the sheep and vines." It's a wonder God hasn't struck me down for my impertinence.

· 800 AD ·

I HAD MY FIRST GLIMPSE OF A POPE ON A BITINGLY COLD spring morning, when Leo rode from the Lateran to the Holy See for the Festival of Saint Mark. Leo was a foreigner, the son of Atyuppius—a Saracen or Slav. He had tricked some virgins into drinking pig's blood from the holy chalice and one of them had given birth to an aurochs with horns. Still, he was Peter's successor, a man intimate with God. His face, I assumed, must radiate a wonderful light.

I had no father to hoist me on his shoulders above the towering Lombards, so I left my dorm before dawn, when the city still belonged to the devil, crossed the river, and made my way through the silent streets to the monastery church of Saints Stephen and Silvester. From here, I could watch the Holy Father as he rode to the old Church of Saint Lorenzo. It was here the formal procession began.

The air was nippy. I relaxed my muscles and told myself I wasn't cold. The pure young voices of the choirboys floated on the morning air, lifting me to a world beyond care. I was about to slip into the church when I heard the distant singing of the Kyrie Eleison. The public seldom joined in, but today was different.

The poor from the hospitals came first, niddle-noddling along the broken streets, holding their painted wooden crosses above their heads. Boys my age came next, followed by the clerical officers and acolytes, the chief officer of the guards, and the regional notaries. Some of them were draped in the silky white robes that Roman officers wore in the days of the Empire.

"Lord have mercy on us," they sang.

"Lord have mercy on us," we cried back.

Then I saw him, the Supreme Pontiff, the Nourisher of the One Immaculate Dove, slouching forward on a large brown horse. As he passed by—so close we could almost touch—the mount in front of him stopped to drop a load, and Leo's horse drew up short. The Pope lurched forward and grabbed the animal's mane to keep from falling. I saw his small pouting mouth, his thin tight lips, his narrow shoulders. I thought his eyes would be shining with God's light, but they were black and empty. I expected to behold the power and the glory, but all I saw was an old man clinging to a startled horse.

Suddenly, a gang of ruffians rushed out from the church, brandishing knives and heavy sticks. The crowd screamed and scattered. The Pope's unarmed guards whirled about on their frightened horses. Leo was seized from his mount and thrown down on the paving stones. No one tried to save him. His face was ripped open. I wanted to wave a sword and shout, "It's me, Augustus," but all I did was stand and watch. And then, God forgive me, I wanted to pummel him, too, this man with terror in his eyes, who feared death more than he loved life; I wanted to slam my fist in his face. As his supporters dragged him into the church, I drew a finger through his blood pooling on the paving stones, and wiped it on my lips. Surely I'm damned, I thought. There is no penance great enough for this.

What Leo's enemies had in store for him I'll never know, because that same night he was lowered by ropes into the arms of the waiting chamberlain and carried to Saint Peter's. Two of King Charles's representatives were in residence there, investigating accusations of adultery and incompetence against the Pope, and one of them set off for Aachen immediately with his wounded charge.

I lay awake that night, among the sleeping boys, struggling with the truth of what I had seen. If the Pope was God's elect, why had God abandoned him? Was it because Leo had fornicated with the devil?

I awoke, moaning for help. Cocks were crowing. I bolted up and thought, "If Leo's guards had been armed, he would have been spared. God is our strength and our shield, but it helps to have a sword."

I lay back, exhausted. I had touched some deep, abiding truth and, cradling it tightly, I fell into a deep, abiding sleep. I was still sleeping when the bells rang for Prime. I dressed quickly and ran to catch up with the others.

TWO

◆——————◆——————◆

LEO RETURNED TO ROME IN LATE NOVEMBER, ESCORTED BY CHARLES'S AGENTS, AND ISO-LATED HIMSELF IN THE LATERAN. HE SELDOM appeared in public anymore, but he continued to sell holy offices to the highest bidder, and one of the virgins he touched gave birth to a frog.

Rumors spread that Charles himself was coming to Rome to look into the accusations against the Pope, but nothing was certain until the king reached Ravenna, accompanied by his son Pippin, king of the Lombards. Though he was a grown man in his thirties, Pippin barely reached up to his father's chest. When he and Charles arrived in Nomentum, twelve milestones from Rome, Leo was there to greet them. No pontiff had ever extended himself so slavishly before.

Word spread that Christmas Mass, usually held at the Church of Santa Maria Maggiore, was moving to Saint Peter's.

Something big was going on. Twenty-six years before, Charles had approached the Eternal City on foot. Now he arrived by horse, accompanied by a grand procession. I found a good vantage point on the steps leading to the grand courtyard. The singing began as a distant hum, and grew to a roar. As the king approached, we surged forward. "Long life to Charles," we shouted. "Victory to the most excellent, crowned of God, mighty and peaceful, king of the Franks and the Lombards, patrician of the Romans."

Charles's hair stuck out, white and unruly, beneath his gold crown. His neck was thick as an oak. He sat squarely on his horse. No one could question who was master. Then, in one smooth, deliberate gesture, he dismounted and slid to the ground. I could have followed him forever.

"Redeemer of the World, help him," the people cried, and I cried too: "Saint Mary, Saint Michael, Saint Gabriel, Saint Raphael, Saint John, Saint Stephen, help him."

His height was amazing. He loomed over everyone. I had expected to see him in a short tunic and high boots, but he was wearing Roman dress: a long green chlamys and the sandals of a nobleman. The jewels on his silver scabbard gleamed in the sun. I imagined him drawing his sword and impaling a charging boar in one clean thrust.

Here is a man who loves and hates, I thought. Here is a man who says yes and no.

"Hear us O Christ," I sang out. "Long life to the most noble family of kings. Holy Virgin of Virgins, help him. Saint Silvester, Saint Laurence, Saint Pancras, help him."

I fought back tears. It was wrong of me to cry, but how could I help myself? I was lifted up on a sea of voices. There was no Deusdona anymore; I merged with the crowd. I bit my lip so the pain would exceed the joy.

"Hear us, O Christ," I shouted. "Long life and victory to all the army of the Franks. Saint Hilary, help them. Saint Martin, Saint Maurice, Saint Denis, help them."

The marble stairway was slippery from an early morning rain, but Charles, who had lived for nearly sixty winters, moved firmly up the steps. I followed him to the great Court of Honor, where he greeted the Pope and the officers of his household. The sky was a deep blue, the day as crisp as a Gozmaringa apple.

Charles and Leo led the procession to the Great Fountain. Here they paused to purify themselves before entering God's house. I should have cleansed myself, too. I should have dipped my hands in the holy water and pressed it to my lips. But I was afraid of losing sight of Charles, and so, like a willful child, I slipped through the great brass doors and pushed my way down the aisle. When I reached the choir I turned, and there, standing in the great doorway, blocking the sun, was Charles.

Benedictus qui venit in nomine Domini. Our voices hummed like bees.

Charles handed his crown and sword to an attendant, bowed, and strode forward. My heart raced as he came toward me. White and purple banners floated between the great columns, flecked with gold. The flames of a thousand candles glanced off the silver beams and candelabras and turned the silver plates before the altar into pools of burning light. Everything shimmered, everything blazed with heavenly fire. This is Peter's home, I thought. He is with us today.

Charles, bathed in brightness, passed through the gates into the choir. He knelt and bowed silently at the golden railing before the confession of the blessed Apostle Peter. Pope Leo took his place at the rear of the church, in the chair of Peter's successors. The *suburbicarian* bishops arranged themselves around him.

The solemn mass was about to begin when Leo climbed down from the bishop's throne, walked around behind the kneeling king, and placed a crown on his head. "To Charles," he cried. "To the most pious Augustus, crowned by God, the great and peace-giving emperor of the Romans: life and victory."

"Long life and victory to Charles Augustus," we shouted back. "Long life and victory to Charles Augustus!"

My heart was bursting. After more than three centuries, we had an emperor again. The crown of the Imperial Caesars was back in Rome.

Smoke from the candles curled up toward the angels in the choir. I shuddered. Eight hundred years ago today God had given us His only Son. Now he was giving us Charles, the *caput orbis*, who would restore Rome to her ancient glory, under Him.

Charles rose and turned to face us. A shadow of grief seemed to cross his face. Was he bruised by the memory of his wife Liutgarda, who had died the previous spring? Perhaps he realized that there is no crown but the crown of glory, no victory but the triumph over death. He flicked his hair from his eyes. Leo anointed him with holy oil and wrapped him in a purple mantle, then prostrated himself, touching his forehead to the ground three times.

I longed to bow down and serve Charles, too. He was not a man but a force, like thunder or a great wind. He straddled the world. He was the current in the Tiber, sweeping all before him.

THREE

◆——————◆——————◆

A FEW DAYS AFTER THE CORONATION, THE POPE'S ENEMIES WERE BANISHED TO GAUL, A PUNISHMENT WORSE THAN DEATH, AND I WENT BACK to my daily duties at the church. Life, like the Tiber, drifted on. Our emperor returned to his palace in Aachen. He seemed very far away.

I passed quickly through the minor orders—from lector to acolyte to subdeacon, where I continued my education for the priesthood. One of my earliest tasks was keeping watch over the *secretarium,* where vessels and vestments are stored between services. Once, finding myself alone, I slipped into a priest's cassock, uncovered the gold chalice that holds the Precious Blood, and, raising it high, cried out, "Blessed are those called to the supper of the Lamb." I had done wrong, and to expiate my sin, I flogged myself and fasted for three days and nights.

Among my other responsibilities was ringing the bell for the morning office, the ancient office of the dawn. More than once the *primicerius* had to storm into my dorm and throw me out of bed. Disheveled, bloated with sleep, I would rush off to prepare the wine for the sacrifice of the Mass, and light the sacred candles on the altar. After the service, I helped clean up. When no one was looking, I licked drops of sweet wine from the priest's gilded cup, and chewed the blackened candlewicks, which were holy. I also swallowed the hot wax, blistering my throat and tongue. I asked God to know my pain, and to forgive me for being me.

Pilgrims arrived daily with offerings from every corner of the world. One of my jobs was to sort through these gifts and set aside whatever was perishable—eggs, say, or snails. Non-perishables I stored in separate boxes allocated for the clergy or the poor.

Visitors, hoping to be rewarded with miracles, showered us with everything from liturgical vessels to embroidered vestments, flowers, clothes, sandals, wax, coins, chickens, sacks of grain, and beans. We accepted everything. No gift was too large or small.

As an acolyte, one of my favorite chores was cleaning the crumbs from the altar after the celebration of the Eucharist. Priests ate leavened bread then, which they broke and shared with the faithful. It made an awful mess.

One day a bishop named Saturninus developed an unleavened bread that could be pressed into a kind of crude wafer and placed directly on the supplicant's tongue. This disturbed me to no end. I had always thought of the Eucharist as a reenactment of the Last Supper, a breaking of bread at a communal meal. Suddenly, with the introduction of this hard round wafer, the priest and I no longer sat together as a loving family at the supper of the Lord. I had never had a family. I had hoped the priesthood would give me one.

PSALMS, SONGS OF PRAISE: IN A MORE SPIRITUAL AGE, in the days of the early Church, we would have recited them all in a day. Now we struggled to get through them in a week. My favorite service was the night office, shortly after midnight, when the only light in the world came from the tapers in the chapel where we prayed, enveloped in darkness, and the cross above the altar branded us with the power of Christ's love. My heart danced as the tiny flames licked the sweet air, heavy with the cloying, comforting smell of cheap oil. I felt a wonderful blind intimacy with my brothers as we sat chanting together on those hard, unforgiving benches, holding the devil at bay with our pale perfumed voices.

Lauds, however, was another matter: How I dreaded being pried from sleep a few hours before dawn and forced to sit shivering in the pre-dawn chill. The devil owned the night then, he made the candles sputter. I was certain he would tear me apart if I fell asleep, and feverishly I prayed for cockcrow and the ordinariness of day.

MY ELDERS ASSUMED I WOULD GO THROUGH MAJOR orders and become a priest. I knew though, even then, that I was unworthy. One day, for instance, when I was suffering from a toothache, I brought the Host home from Mass, hidden against the roof of my mouth, and pounded it into a powder which I drank with a few drops of wine. It worked. The evil spirit fled. But I had committed an unforgiveable sin, and the next Sunday blood flowed from the Host when the priest placed it on my tongue.

I also saw Christ in a way that was anathema to many in the Church, not as a king but as a shepherd tending his flock. To my contemporaries nothing mattered but the divine prerogative: the Father, not the Son. Alone with my heretical thoughts I wandered along the Appian Way, the road on which Peter, the Apostle of the Gentiles, entered Rome, and, finding myself a stick, scratched pictures in the dust of a sweet young Jesus with his slender staff and his seven-stringed lyre.

I WAS TORMENTED BY MY OWN UNWORTHINESS. WHEN the *primicerius* lectured me on Augustine, he sat me on his lap and stroked my closely cropped hair; and as he contrasted the perishing Roman state to the heavenly City of God, I felt an unholy stirring in me.

When he left for Lyon—there was a commentary on the curative powers of pain he wanted to consult—he kissed me hard on the lips, with the sound of clapping hands or thunder. And during his three-month absence he flooded me with letters.

"I think of your friendship with such sweet memories," he wrote, "that I long for the time when I may be able to clutch the neck of your sweetness with the fingers of your desires."

Another time he wrote: "If I could be with you, how I would sink into your embraces, how I would cover, with tightly pressed lips, your eyes, ears, and mouth, every finger and toe, not once but many times. I ever lick your breast and wish to wash, beloved, your chest with my tears."

I was touched, roused, punished, and tested by his words. I counted the days until I would see him again. When at last he returned he was a mere shadow of the man I once knew. He looked tortured, possessed. I hardly recognized him. For days he lived only on water. His condition deteriorated. At night he slept in the frigid church or on a bed of nettles. Once, I'm told, he passed the night with a corpse in a grave. That he ignored me, that he sometimes failed to recognize me, I attributed to his illness. But one day, finding me alone, he instructed me to burn his letters, and spoke with such reproach in his voice that I could almost hear him whisper, "Get behind me, Satan."

Later that day I removed a small pile of letters from under my mattress, wrapped them in a plane tree root, and went in search of him. I found him alone in the chapel, rolling on the floor below the altar, grinding his teeth and foaming at the mouth.

"Mark tells us that prayers can save us, even from the jaws of death," I told him. He looked up but couldn't find me. "The letters," I said, placing them before him. "I didn't have the heart to burn them."

I turned and left. He died that same day. Possessed by the devil, he was denied a proper burial and set on fire. I could say he disappeared from my life, but that wouldn't be true. Many years later, on one of my business trips across the Alps, I found all of my teacher's letters to me in the Lyon library, collected under the name of Charles's court scholar Alcuin. The *primicerius* must have copied them on one of his visits to Lyon and passed them off to me as his own. Not that it matters. If all comes from God, how can anything be called our own?

I had a final encounter with the *primicerius* a year later. He visited me on a moonlit night, wakening me from a deep sleep. I had to scream to make him go away. Sitting up in bed, I tried to understand what I could have done to defile him. All I knew was that his eyes bound me in chains from which I'm still struggling to break free.

FOUR

T WAS ABOUT THIS TIME THAT GOD LED ME TO THE CATACOMBS. I WAS WANDERING ALONG THE VIA LABICANA LATE ONE DAY, NOT FAR FROM SAINT John's Gate, when a downpour sent me scurrying to some ancient ruins for cover. Pushing my way through the high, tangled grasses, I came to a large, roofless basilica overgrown with nettles. As I stepped among the cypress and gray-leaved ilex, I noticed a flight of slick, moss-covered steps, disappearing into the ground. I hesitated, but the rain was sharp and cold, so I asked God to protect me, and descended.

Dim lights flickered in the crypt below. The air smelled sickly sweet, like an overripe melon. The dampness cut through me like iron. Suddenly I was standing in a low-arched chamber, before a marble altar. The walls were covered with religious scenes, barely distinguishable in the gloom. The mensa was strewn with wilted flowers, blood-red and white.

Suddenly I froze. There in the corner was the twisted body of a demon, gaping up at me through lidless eyes. I turned and fled up the stairs, through the wet grasses, back to the Via Labicana. I pulled off my tunic as I ran. The rain lashed me like a whip.

THE ALTAR, I LEARNED FROM A PRIEST, COVERED THE earthly remains of two holy Roman martyrs, Peter and Marcellinus, who had been persecuted in the time of Diocletian. The steps offered a shortcut to their tomb.

When the skies cleared I paid the martyrs a second visit, this time with my classmate Luniso. He had never deigned to spend time with me before, but my hair-raising adventure intrigued him.

He lit a torch at the entrance and, without a prayer or a moment's hesitation, plunged down into the ground. I touched the small box of relics that hung from my neck, and followed close behind. Our warm breath bloomed in the chilly air like poisonous white flowers. Tuber-like roots grew down through cracks in the plaster ceiling. Drops of moisture hung from them like jewels. Flames leaped from two or three oil lamps left by the faithful, blackening the walls. The sacred bones sweetened the air with the clean, spicy scent of frankincense and myrrh.

Luniso pointed gleefully at the partly decomposed body of a sheep, which must have wandered down into the crypt and lost its way.

"So much for your demon," he laughed.

Nothing fazed Luniso. He hummed as he paced off the marble floor: fifteen feet by twenty-five. Pieces of fluted marble lay about an opening in the far left wall. "That should be the original entrance, through the catacombs," he announced. "Let's go see."

He lifted his torch and headed down the narrow corridor. I rushed after him. The dead slept in niches dug into the rough walls, one above the other, five or six bodies high. A few tombs remained sealed behind tiles or marble slabs, but most of them had been plundered over the centuries by grave robbers. I reached into a gaping black hole and touched a bone. It crumbled in my hand like ash.

Whenever Luniso turned a corner, he left me in total darkness. An owl hooted. A bat rushed by my head. Luniso laughed. What did he know that made him so unafraid of death?

On we went. The air tasted old. Our shadows leaped across the walls like sprites. I was terrified that we would lose our way like the hapless sheep and be found hundreds of years from now, bones and dust.

It would be an honor, I mused, dying beside Luniso, our names forever linked on peoples' lips.

STOOPING THROUGH A LOW, LONELY CORRIDOR, WE found ourselves in a family crypt decorated with scenes of hope and redemption, life beyond this vale of tears. One of the paintings, severely damaged by water, portrayed a Roman family gathered around a table, sharing a joyful evening meal.

The scene still haunts me. Agape and Irene—Love and Peace—stand behind a table, waiting to serve the fish and wine—the flesh and blood of Christ. *Misce me!* says the father. Mix the wine for me. *Da calda.* Make it warm. The parents and children slouch forward in easy conversation, their arms and elbows on the table. It is a banquet of the blessed, a celebration of the Eucharist as it was meant to be observed: as an ordinary family meal.

Luniso stepped back into the dreary passageway, waving his lantern. The darkness enveloped me. I lunged after him. How far he would have led me I'll never know, for God in His mercy blocked our way with debris fallen through a skylight, and forced us to retrace our steps. We passed back through the chapel of Peter and Marcellinus, up into the blinding light of day.

FIVE

I MASTERED MY SCRIBAL SKILLS WITH AN EASE MY FATHER WOULD HAVE HUGGED ME FOR, AND WENT TO WORK IN THE *SCRINIARIUM* AS ONE OF HUN-dreds of glorified young notaries overseeing the daily business of the Church. Having a way with words, I was assigned to the library, where I handled requests for books and kept records of those on loan.

"We search for Cicero's *De Oratore* and the *Commentaries of Donatus on Terence*," wrote an elderly monk from Lorsch. "Please also send us the *Commentaries of Saint Jerome on Jeremiah*, from the seventh book to the end. We'll return it as soon as it's copied. We can't find anything beyond the sixth book north of the Alps."

Four months passed before I could find a messenger going to Lorsch whom I could entrust these treasures to. Did he drown on the way? Was he waylaid by robbers or eaten by wild beasts?

I'll never know. Neither he nor the books he was charged to deliver were ever seen again.

On dark nights, when I'm fast sleep, I still sometimes pay a visit to the monk from Lorsch. I find him sitting on the floor of his cold dark cell, waiting for the scraps of ancient wisdom I tried to send him. I call out to him but he doesn't answer. Animals without names howl outside his door. The only light is the lamp he reads by and the stars.

I ENVIED THE POPE'S MESSENGERS THEIR FREEDOM, their availability for whatever life threw their way. When I wasn't working in the library, I wandered over to Saint Peter's stables and helped the boys load the carts and harness the horses as they set off around the kingdom. I was still waving long after they rumbled out of sight.

A horse named Romulus, a strong Low Country horse with Oriental blood, would follow me around the stables, nuzzling me and licking honey from my fingers with his rough tongue. His power was astonishing. When his hooves began to split and soften, I pleaded with the count of the stable to give him wooden shoes. He wouldn't hear of it. "You bookish types are all alike," he growled. "If horses were meant to have shoes, God would have given them shoes." Romulus whinnied and pawed the ground. He could hardly stand. A few weeks later the count had him slaughtered.

SIX

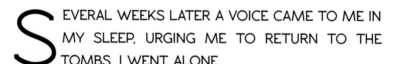

S EVERAL WEEKS LATER A VOICE CAME TO ME IN MY SLEEP, URGING ME TO RETURN TO THE TOMBS. I WENT ALONE.

As I felt my way along the dim, dank corridors, I was surprised by the absence of images of pain and torture. A gentle Jesus played his lute in a garden, taming the hearts of man and beast, drowning the world in sweetness. Lambs gamboled. Doves floated on the still air. What I saw—what God had led me to—was a world of quiet joy and peace, beyond suffering, where compassion triumphed over death. Persecution had no victims here.

I LEARNED WHAT I COULD ABOUT PETER AND MAR-CELLINUS, but there was little anyone could tell me. Marcellinus had been a priest, leading men to God. Peter was an exorcist, fighting the devils that hide in our closets and under our beds, claiming us at night. An exorcist is younger, usually just starting his training for the priesthood, so the smaller bones must have been Peter's.

The two Christians were beheaded for their faith during the reign of Pope Damasus, the thirty-fifth pope after Saint Peter. The executioner led them to a thicket overgrown with thorns and briars, where no one was likely to find them. Cheerfully, the martyrs went to work clearing space for their graves, then offered their necks to the executioner's blade. They were buried on the spot, and would have been lost to us if two pious ladies, Lucilla and Firmina, hadn't found their bodies and arranged to have them transferred to the chapel *ad duas lauros* (at the two laurel trees), along the Via Labicana, a short walk south of the city walls. They were buried in niches in the earth, one above the other, wrapped only in shrouds. Damasus learned all the particulars from the mouth of the executioner himself, who subsequently converted.

I explained all this to Luniso one afternoon, but he barely listened. This was today; the catacombs were yesterday. What had he to do with death?

SEVEN

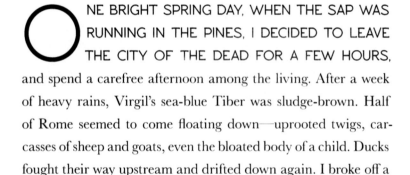

ONE BRIGHT SPRING DAY, WHEN THE SAP WAS RUNNING IN THE PINES, I DECIDED TO LEAVE THE CITY OF THE DEAD FOR A FEW HOURS, and spend a carefree afternoon among the living. After a week of heavy rains, Virgil's sea-blue Tiber was sludge-brown. Half of Rome seemed to come floating down—uprooted twigs, carcasses of sheep and goats, even the bloated body of a child. Ducks fought their way upstream and drifted down again. I broke off a dead branch and tossed it into the current and watched it float under the Ponte Sant'Angelo and out to sea.

Then I stepped through the gates and entered the Imperial City, as Caesar had done, and Peter, and Charles. Massive chunks of brick had fallen from the mighty walls, exposing the rubble beneath. Grass grew on the ramparts. Bird droppings stained the stones where sentries once stood, guarding the capital of the world. I shuddered. If Rome's walls couldn't keep out the barbarians, there was no way to be safe. Night, sickness, death—anything could enter. There was no place to hide except in God's hands.

A church bell rang. These bells keep devils away, I mused. Imagine a bell, stronger than the walls of Rome.

WHEREVER I WENT, WORKERS WERE BUSY TEARING DOWN Imperial Rome and replacing it with the City of God. My teachers praised this transformation, but it was wrenching to watch. Streets were piled high with metal ties and clamps ripped from ancient buildings. Porticos were improvised from unmatched shafts and capitals. Ox-drawn carts clattered over the loose stones, hauling slabs of marble from the Temple of Minerva to Pope Leo's new *triclinium*.

At a kiln across from the Pantheon, a crew of squat, stumpy Greeks was busy stuffing a Vestal Virgin into a red-hot furnace, reducing the marble to lime, for plaster. The priests had taught me that God humbled Rome to punish us for our godless ways, and that a greater city was rising from the ruins. But the burning of these immaculate limbs, these firm white breasts, seemed a kind of desecration.

LIKE OUR FALLEN CITY, I HAD NO CROWN TO LOSE, NO power to usurp, so I wandered through the ancient streets, as free as a beggar. At the Pantheon I turned right and headed toward the Palatine. The dust from passing carts was thick enough to choke on. Old women sat in their windows, dressed in black, like crows. I turned away from their derisive laughter and headed to Trajan's Forum, where Jews from Lyon were auctioning off some Bulgar girls. God had favored them with physical beauty, if you could ignore the gaps between their teeth. A blind man was reciting Virgil. I edged close to him, knowing he couldn't see me peering into his sunken eyes. I had never liked Aeneas—he had run out on his wife, something a real hero wouldn't do—but the portrait of him embracing his father's ghost reminded me of the father I never knew, and left me close to tears.

I can still remember Aeneas' words:

> *Your ghost,*
> *Your sad ghost, father, often before my mind,*
> *Impelled me to the threshold of this place.*

> *My ships ride anchored in the Tuscan Sea.*
> *But let me have your hand, let me embrace you,*
> *Do not draw back.*

> *At this his tears brimmed over*
> *And down his cheeks. And there he tried three times*
> *To throw his arms around his father's neck.*
> *Three times the shade untouched slipped through his hands,*
> *Weightless as wind and fugitive as dream.*

I needed to be alone with my feelings, so I raced to the market, tripping over broken flagstones along the way. It was here, among the traders of the world, that I spent my happiest hours. Smells of the East—cinnamon, cloves, camphor, musk—rose from every alleyway. Each sight, each sensation pierced me with an almost pagan joy.

A pride of clerics poked their fingers through a pile of purple fabrics, searching for their Sunday bests. A black man with pink hands squatted in the dust with his swan quills, scratching out letters and prayers for the cost of a loaf of bread. Burgundians reeking of garlic and onions sold sheepskins and furs. Greeks sat at tables piled high with pistachios. I found one of these exotic nuts lying on the street and sucked the sweetness from its salty flesh.

A swarthy-skinned Jew squatted beside a bag of camphor, promising to cure the world's itches and pains. He barked his message in a dozen tongues. A man from the East, with a growth on his neck the size of a cantaloupe, tried to sell me a vial of oil from the Church of the Holy Sepulchre in Jerusalem. If only I had had the courage to talk to him, what amazing stories I would have heard.

I kept my distance from a penitent bound in chains who claimed he hadn't washed for seventeen years. His smell would have sent the devil packing. An old woman blind in one eye swung a dead vulture around her head, screeching, "This bird was killed with a sharp reed, not a knife. Mix the brain with good oil, rub it in your nose, and your migraines will go away. Put its tongue in your right shoe and your enemies will love you."

There was a world out there that was different from my own, that was sure; a place so strange and foreign that its sun must give off a different light.

IT WAS IN THE VENETIAN QUARTER OF THE MARKET THAT I saw my face for the first time, starring back at me in a sheet of polished brass. I had seen my image in water, of course, but never in a mirror. Who is this tonsured boy? I wondered. Great Romans have strong, angular noses; mine is weak and fleshy. No Roman senator ever had such watery lips.

The truth pierced me like a nail.

EIGHT

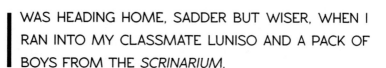

I WAS HEADING HOME, SADDER BUT WISER, WHEN I RAN INTO MY CLASSMATE LUNISO AND A PACK OF BOYS FROM THE *SCRINARIUM.*

"Crabs for sale," Luniso shouted, taunting a cripple with stumps for legs and hands.

We laughed as we wove our way through the tenements, up to the foot of the Palatine, across from the Field of Mars.

Free from the tyranny of priests, we pushed each other into piles of steaming excrement, and splashed in streams of piss running down the wagon ruts. Armed with sticks, we became Roman legionnaires driving the Carthaginians from Sicily, or Israelites laying siege to Jericho.

We pulled ourselves up the broken steps of an abandoned apartment building and played in the debris. Luniso threw a stone at a fair-haired boy named Theodulf, a Frank, and drew blood. We laughed. Theodulf was too stupid to read the penitentials or martyrologies, and wore his hair long, like a girl. "Happy the nose that cannot smell a barbarian," said Luniso, showing us his bright white teeth.

Wrestling came next. This was my sport; I loved the touching. There was something blind and disembodied about it. It wasn't Deusdona against Sergius, we were both part of a single hard warm ball of flesh and muscle, rearranging itself. I didn't have to tell my body what to do, it acted on its own.

I lost, I won.

THEN WE CLIMBED PAST THE TOWERING CYPRESS TREES, lining the Royal Way like flaming green torches, and slipped into the shadow of the Arch of Titus. Half the emperor's head was gone. His horse's leg was missing. When we stepped back into the sinking sun, the ancient city spread out before us, brushed with gold. A shepherd led his sheep through the rough grasses, as in Evander's time. I stumbled on a child's skull. It may have been unbaptized, or dragged from its grave by a devil, but I didn't wait around long enough to find out.

As we ran to the Arch of Septimius Severus, I jumped on a broken pedestal, brandished my stick, and shouted, "It's me, Augustus!" No one noticed. No one cared.

Luniso and another classmate jumped on opposite ends of a fallen pillar and approached each other like gladiators. I joined the boys cheering them on. Luniso won, of course. He was invincible. He was a brute, but we loved him. He was entirely himself. Nothing stood between him and the day.

As our shadows lengthened, we jumped on them, squealing with fear. Luniso was in no hurry to leave, so we lingered. He was in the mood for hide-and-seek, so we scattered across the Palatine. I ran and hid behind a shattered pillar, held my breath, and asked God to turn me into stone or sky. I waited what seemed a lifetime. No one came.

When I peered out, I was alone, away from the boasting boys. Everyone had gone. A lizard darted through the shadows, flicking its tongue. I was alone on the hill among the ruins of a dead world. A church bell rang. It was the voice of God, calling me home. I hurried back for Vespers.

NINE

◆——————◆——————◆

ONE MOONLESS NIGHT, NEAR MY THIRTEENTH BIRTH DAY, A VOICE CAME TO ME IN BED, ADVISING ME TO LEAVE THE LIBRARY AND serve God in the catacombs. There are seven cemeterial districts in Rome. I was appointed assistant to the deacon in charge of the third, an area encompassing the Prenestina, Tibertina, and Labicana. The catacomb of Peter and Marcellinus was in the Labicana.

It was my job to lead dignitaries and groups of pilgrims through the ancient passages and pray with them at the holiest shrines. Guidebooks and itineraries were useless here; visitors were lost without me. I felt a rush of pleasure as I led them down the dark, damp corridors. Sinners and sycophants, abbots and acolytes, merchants and thieves—everyone clustered around my light.

I spent my free time trying to preserve this crumbling world. I filled fonts with holy water, and lamps with sweet-smelling oils. I broke off the roots of trees that were growing down through the ceilings, cracking plaster, destroying priceless paintings, and wrapping themselves around the bones of our holiest protectors. I swept up dead rodents and cleared walkways choked with rubbish. People said that jackals and wolves lived here, but I never saw one. Several times I stumbled on a debtor or thief who made his home in an abandoned chapel, but they were always more frightened than I was, and scurried off into the darkness.

It was in one of the Jewish catacombs, standing among the circumcised dead, that I fornicated with myself. I was sure that, like Onan, I would be struck down for spilling my seed, but God is merciful and He let me earn forgiveness on a diet of stale bread and water.

I also defiled myself in my sleep, but this was not a sin, as we have no defense against the devil when we are sleeping. When the urge to sully myself returned, I denied myself, thanks to God. No land can bear fruit which in a single year is frequently sown, sacred scripture tells us, so why would we do to our bodies what we wouldn't do to our own fields?

At about this time I began selling amulets to believers, which they wore around their necks to guard against sickness and death. The most popular were lead badges, which are still sold in the shrines, engraved with the image of Christ mounted on a horse, bearing a cross. Pilgrims couldn't get enough of them, so I bought a large supply from a Greek priest and sold them at a hefty profit. I donated my first piece of silver to the poor. With the second I bought a bag of pistachios.

I also sold priceless guidebooks to the wealthiest pilgrims, who, in their ignorance, believed a visit to a shrine increased the chances of eternal life. "The only guide you need is faith," I wanted to say. "The journey to God is inward. You can also find Him without leaving home."

TO BRING LIGHT TO A DARK WORLD, AND TO MAKE A LIV-ing, I swept dust from the holy tombs into tiny cloth packets and sold them to pilgrims. I also sold strips of sanctified cloth that had touched the relics, and vials of lamp oil that lit the chapels.

Some believers pressed coins into my hands, often their life savings, hoping to purchase a sliver of bone or a pinch of holy dust that would open the gates of heaven. I always turned them down. Monks tried to bribe me with prayers and the promise of eternal life, but I ignored them, too. Rome's holiest protectors were not for sale. I guarded them as a man guards his family from murderers and thieves.

Though I would never deliberately sell a sacred bone, I did over time agree to part with some of the holy objects that were identified with, or had come in touch with, the saints and martyrs.

I sold three drops of blood from the Crucifixion to a pious baker from the Low Country, and his barren wife gave birth to a child before he returned home. Pilgrims from Ireland bought angel meat from me by the pound, and spread it on the ground, resulting in a bumper crop of vetches. A bearded Frisian bought a spoonful of the manna God gave the Israelites in the wilderness. The Franks took whatever I offered them: pieces of the clay from which God shaped Adam, slivers of Aaron's rod, thorns from the holy crown.

I once sold a Spanish abbot a chipped water pot that was used at Cana, strands of the Virgin's hair in shades of red, black, brown, and yellow, and enough of the Virgin Mother's milk to feed a baby for a year. God rewarded me with a good living and excellent health.

Nothing was in greater demand than wood from the Cross. Buyers could be very demanding, though. An old Semite from Jerusalem once sent back a stick of boxwood, insisting that the True Cross was made of palm. He cursed me in God's name.

TEN

◆——————◆——————◆

· 805–806 AD ·

I FOUND MY TRUE CALLING THE DAY I BEGAN SELL-
ING THE BONES OF SAINTS AND MARTYRS—NOT
THE REAL ONES, OF COURSE, BUT SUBSTITUTES,
replacements. The actual relics, the originals, I moved to
unmarked graves in the darkest corners of the catacombs,
where they continued to perform miracles, safe from the grasp-
ing hands of popes and kings.

My timing couldn't have been more opportune. Frankish
missionaries were busy spreading Christianity among the Saxons
and Avars, and no church or chapel could be sanctified until a
relic was buried below the altar.

Of all the relics, none performed more spectacular miracles or attracted more pilgrim silver than the bones of early
Christians—saints who lived for God, and martyrs who died for

Him. A Frankish lord or abbot paid a king's ransom to own one. It was a major investment, but it paid off long-term.

I spent the winter rummaging through the catacombs, digging up worthless bones I could sell as priceless relics. When Hildoin, the abbot of Saint Médard, asked for several of Saint Sebastian's ribs, I brought him three worthless bones from a pauper's grave, and threw in a few broken arrows for effect. The ignorant still believe Sebastian died from arrow wounds, when in fact he was bludgeoned to death with a club. But if they expected arrows, I wasn't going to disappoint them. Arrow it would be.

Hildoin should have known he was getting fakes for another, more obvious reason. All true relics assault our senses with the smell of exotic spices or the sweet perfume of roses, daffodils, and other heavenly flowers. The ribs I gave him had a musty smell. If they had been genuine, they would have pulsated in the dark with a soft, blue light. They wouldn't have just lain there like old bones.

I found the ribs in less time than it takes to say, *"in nomine patris et filii et spiritus sancti"*—the father, the son and the Holy Ghost. You don't have to go far for ribs in the City of the Dead.

ELEVEN

MY DAYS BECAME AS PREDICTABLE AND FAMILIAR AS MORNING PRAYERS. EVERY SPRING, AS SOON AS THE SNOWS BEGAN to melt from the alpine passes, I followed the ancient Roman roads north with my cargo of old bones, visiting churches and fairs, filling orders from the previous summer and drumming up business for the year to come. Everyone made out well. The citizens of Rome got to keep their priceless saints and martyrs, who defended them against our enemies. The bones I sold brought the hope of redemption to an ignorant and superstitious people, and reinforced the spiritual centrality of Rome. The relics I sold were worthless as dust, but the Franks believed in their powers and were inspired by them, and who is to say they were wrong or misled?

Thanks to me, the Franks were able to glimpse a world beyond their own. I never owned a sword, but I did the work of a thousand swords, capturing men's hearts and souls, and winning them to God. To the faithful, each relic was a little spark of divine power made manifest on earth—touchable, portable, deeply holy. Did it really matter whose bone it was, if it inspired faith? A God who can feed five thousand with a few small barley loaves can sanctify the middle finger of an impecunious Jew or the broken jaw of an ancient galley slave. Everything is possible with Him. What turns people from Him is wrong. What turns them to Him is right. I tremble at the power of a God who can turn senseless bones and dust into instruments of salvation.

TWELVE

IT WAS NOT MY INVENTORY OF BODY PARTS THAT DISTINGUISHED ME FROM OTHER RELIC DEALERS AND MADE MY REPUTATION. IT WAS THE SPEED OF my transactions. A request made directly to the pope could take months to process and deliver; I could usually turn an order around in a day. I once delivered recognizable parts of eighteen saints and martyrs in a weekend—twelve Dionysiuses, five Julians, three Flavians, and one Xystuses. I needed only five days to deliver limbs of Argus, Smaragdus, Soteris, Parthenius, Calocerus, Nereus, Achilleus, Processus, and Martinian.

I should add that though I could always outperform the pope, I sometimes chose not to. I could have pulled together an order for the abbot of Fulda in three days—he wanted limbs of Alexander, Fabian, Urban, Felicissimus, and Felicity—but I told him I needed three weeks. It was the right decision. Any true man of God will tell you a saint worth having is a saint worth waiting for.

There was no way to authenticate each bone I sold—no official document, inscription, or seal—so customers often had nothing to rely on but my word. My credibility was on the line with every sale. Without it, I might as well have gone into sandals or socks. Fortunately, buyers who questioned my integrity were forced to keep their worries to themselves. Romans made short work of anyone who threatened to steal or buy a saint or martyr. No one who valued his life talked about it.

The worst way to build confidence among my customers, I learned, was to offer them the same celebrated martyrs again and again. When I tried to sell John the Baptist's skull to the Benedictine monk Hrabanus Maurus, he said to me, "Deusdona, how can this be, when the back of the skull is in Constantinople, the forehead is in the Church of Sylvester in Rome, the jaws are in Genoa, and at least one of the teeth is in Vienna?"

"Through their miracles you shall know God's saints," I replied. It was a disingenuous reply, and I began to steer customers to some of our more neglected sons and daughters. The third-century heresiarch Novatian was one of them. I kept his earthly remains in a small, little-known catacomb on the Via Tiburtina near San Lorenzo, and sold him fifty-three times. He was a schismatic, so I let him go for a few pieces of silver.

THOSE WHO QUESTIONED MY INTEGRITY SOMETIMES asked to accompany me to the tombs to verify the relics for themselves. That was their privilege, but I made them pay for it. One of them once memorized the tortuous route to Saint Fabiola's grave, then asked me to lead him there. I rewarded his suspicions by snuffing out my lamp and leaving him in a world so dark and grim, he would have sold his soul to see the sun again. Blindly he groped through the darkness, his mind emptied of every thought but getting out alive.

I WORKED HARD FOR MY SUCCESS. EVERY BONE I SOLD I rubbed with expensive oils from the East. I required only a small deposit, most of which I returned if a relic failed to perform miracles within a designated time. I often sold two saints for less than twice the cost of one. Whatever I sold, I packaged tastefully, to God's delight. While other dealers accepted payment only in gold and silver, I took whatever I was offered of equal value: horn vases, gold baldrics, silk chasubles, silver patens. I traded these in the market or I donated them to welfare centers run by the Church.

EVERY BUYER TRIES TO PROMOTE A NEWLY ACQUIRED relic as it journeys to its new home—the greater the fuss, the better—so for a reasonable fee I would arrange to have the sacred treasure carried on ornamental cars, accompanied by a solemn procession bearing torches and chanting hymns. For cost plus a modest markup, I sent messengers ahead to let villagers know when a saint or martyr was about to pass through, often building expectations to a fever pitch. Where faith was weak, my assistants paid women to writhe on church floors before the altar and then to suddenly recover, enhancing the reputation of the saint. Word of these miracles drew crowds and added to church coffers and to the glory of God.

When the abbot at Corbie complained that Novatian's upper arm was not performing the miracles we had agreed on, I arranged for a young girl to urinate in the churchyard near the altar where the limb was enshrined, and then to remain paralyzed in a squatting position until the townspeople ran to the site and prayed to Novatian to forgive her. The martyr has been performing miracles at Corbie ever since, bringing faith to the unblessed, and silver to the abbot.

One spring I accompanied a rib of the eunuch Nereus partway to his new home in Langres. As we passed from village to village, faces lit up with radiant joy. Men and women stopped their work or play and ran to join us—the strong and healthy, the blind and lame—some of them crawling on withered limbs or dragging themselves along on bloody knees. We distributed colored standards to the children, who waved them as they sang the Kyrie Eleison or the psalms.

What a rush of hope it gave these untutored Franks to know that a saint had deigned to visit, that God had not forsaken them. The martyr, once condemned to death, was now the living judge. Though slaughtered, he had won the battle. As the relic passed before them, the villagers lowered their heads in respect, and crossed themselves. Others tossed flowers on the holy bier or reached out to touch it. I saw their pleading glances, their clasped hands, their looks of silent awe, and my eyes glossed over with contentment. Once, however, just outside Langres, a stooped, gray-haired farmer continued to work his fields, ignoring us as we passed. Was he addle-headed? Did he think we carried only worthless dust? I still see him, alone with his sickle, slicing the grasses like an angel of death.

THIRTEEN

◆——————◆——————◆

E VEN BEFORE DAYLIGHT, I WENT TO WORK EACH
MORNING SORTING THROUGH AND LABELING
MY GROWING COLLECTION OF BONES. THERE
were endless ways to organize them—by name, cost, birthplace,
types of miracles they performed, types of death (violent, natural), body part (arm, foot, leg), and so on. One client had a
perverse—some would say disarming—affection for thumbs,
caring more about their shape and condition than he did about
the saint they came from. Relics associated with a particular
saint or martyr—a hair from the tail of the ass that Jesus rode
into Rome, a link from Peter's chains—I stored in wooden crates
on the upper shelves of my home, so high up, I needed a chair to
reach them. It discouraged snooping.

I sold to buyers who were both new to the business and
long-established. Some sent couriers. Others came alone, or with

associates and friends. Abbots and emperors, with their insatiable lust for relics and their blind, superstitious faith in bones and sacred dust, bought virtually everything I offered them: Matthew's earlobe, John's kneecap, Mary's nose.

God rewarded me with a good living and decent health.

TO WIN A CUSTOMER'S CONFIDENCE, I WORKED HARD ON my dress and demeanor. The face I presented to the world was humble, but not fawning. I bathed at least twice a week when I could, and wore clothes that showed I was prospering, without calling attention to myself. I shared some of my earnings with the lame and the poor. I kept my prices honest. I was not selling combs or goats.

It didn't hurt that I was a Roman citizen in the employ of the Church. It gave me a competitive edge. There were always Doubting Thomases, but even they wanted access to the saints. Believers reached out to me in the same way that a drowning sailor reaches out for the nearest hand and doesn't stop to question whose it is, or to chat about the weather. Felix, a relic monger of no pedigree or consequence, could not compete with me and was forced to establish a smaller territory farther south.

I TRIED TO KEEP OUR SAINTS AND MARTYRS IN ROME, where they could watch over us and keep us from harm in God's name, but they continued to slip into the hands of churchmen and thieves—men like the vain, inglorious archchaplain Hildoin of Saint Médard, who would pay any price to augment his collection. At the rate we were going, Rome's entire Celestial Army would be lost to the Devil, and the Saracens, with no one to stop them, would push us into the sea. God was furious at us for abandoning His soldiers, and turned away in disgust. The Roman people cried out for help. My business grew.

SEASONS PASSED, AND I BECAME LESS OF A BOY AND more of a man. I was fourteen when I first shaved. Two days later the sun grew dark at noon. I gave some silver to the poor and paid seven beggars to undertake a three-day fast in my name.

One day Luniso was playing with us in the Forum, the next he was gone. No one knew where. I would have been surprised if he had stopped to say goodbye, but when I heard of his abrupt departure I felt extinguished, like a taper in a gust of wind. For years we had rallied around him; he had centered us and made us whole. Wherever he was, I was sure boys still formed behind him, cheering wildly as they marched off to victory or defeat.

Without Luniso to anchor us, we drifted apart. The boys who had played hide-and-seek with me became priests. Some, seeking advancement, went to Ravenna or Constantinople, or into abbeys. I began spending more time with Peter and Marcellinus. I also made frequent forays into the marketplace, drawn to a world beyond my own.

· 810 AD ·

NEWS ARRIVED THAT KING CHARLES HAD FALLEN FROM his horse while returning from a campaign against the Danes—an ill omen. Twice the sky turned black at midday, and twice the moon disappeared. At the monastery of Saint Riquier, three hundred and ninety monks and one hundred clerks prayed for the emperor's salvation. They were helped by relics of fifty-five martyrs, thirty-five confessors, and fourteen virgins.

Charles kept countless relics in his chapel, behind the Altar to the Virgin. He could not get enough. There was a new urgency now to his demands, and Pope Leo instructed his chief notary to prepare a shipment for the failing emperor. The notary quickly gathered an assortment of forty-two additional saints and martyrs. To these he added a cutting from Jesus's umbilical cord, and a strip of the loincloth Christ wore to his crucifixion.

Charles was an old man now. If I wanted to see him again, it had to be now. I approached the Pope through one of his notaries, and petitioned him to let me accompany his emissaries to Aachen. He not only consented, he instructed me to carry the priceless treasure myself, in a wagon that never leaked, even in a raging stream. Wrapped in leather and sealed with wax, pitch, and tow, it was a miracle of modern design.

I spent my last night in Rome alone with Peter and Marcellinus. "I'm not abandoning you," I told them. "We serve the same God. I'll be back before you know it." Then I lay down beside them and fell asleep in their embrace.

Early the next morning I climbed back into the light. The west wind was blowing, a good omen. The earth was stirring. A farmer and his wife walked side by side, spreading ashes on their exhausted fields. They didn't see me waving. Their son, a boy half my age, squatted on a log, feeding arbutus leaves to a baby goat. An old man sat beside him, turning an elm branch into a plough beam.

Seven wagons were waiting for me at Saint Peter's stables. I harnessed up. The horses were restless.

"It's time," someone said.

FOURTEEN

◆———◆———◆

WE LURCHED ACROSS THE GREAT PLAINS UNDER AN ENORMOUS SKY. THE ROAD HAD A LIFE OF ITS OWN. VENETIAN MERCHANTS rolled past us on their way to the great fair in Aachen, their wagons overflowing with silks. We traveled on official business for the Holy See, but farmers ignored us as they trudged to abbeys and manor houses to work off their debts. Half-naked Slavs lumbered toward the slave markets in Rome. A boy half my age waved at me as I rattled past. I looked away. He would go for about one hundred and seventy denier, half the cost of a good horse.

We followed a well-worn route, jolting our way west from Piacenza to Pavia, where we loaded up on provisions: wine, wheat, dried grapes, plums, salted pork, and a new kind of hard bread, well-preserved, called a biscuit. Then on to Vercelli, Ivrea, and Aosta, along the Via Flaminia.

There were tolls for everything—safe conduct, road repair, pack animals, wagons, nuts. Pope Leo provided us with a letter exempting us from taxes as we passed through papal lands, but most toll collectors couldn't read, and wouldn't let us pass without a gift of baptismal water from Saint Peter's, or some other sacred bribe.

It took three weeks for us to reach Aosta, a distance of about five hundred miles. We could have gone faster, but my horse was old and forever stopping to nibble on clover, ignoring his master as the body ignores the soul. I called him Romulus, in memory of the horse that used to follow me around the royal stables.

THIS WAS MY FIRST TRIP AWAY FROM HOME, AND I WAS awed by the bounty of God's world.

We were never hungry. Ducks, swans, storks, herons—we had our choice. We gorged on hedgehog and squirrel, boiling the meat the way the Franks do, with garlic and mushrooms, and making soup from the juices thickened with flour or barley. We cut our food on a plate made of unleavened bread, and then we soaked the plate with soup and ate it too. I loved the delicate, slightly gamey taste of starlings, though they took forever to prepare and always left me hungry. A Spanish merchant from Barcelona taught us to appreciate rabbit. The Franks wouldn't touch them, so they were ours for the taking.

Acorns are a poor man's food, but I loved gathering them, grinding them into flour, and baking them in the embers of the fire, stuffed with wild cranberries that exploded tartly in my mouth. From farmsteads we bought fennel, cabbage, leeks, beans, and lentils. Endive, with its crunchy, slightly bitter taste, was always a treat when we could find it.

We feasted on deer, rabbit, scrawny black pigs scrounging for beechmast. We boiled sassafras roots for tea and stained our tongues with the juice of wild mountain ash berries. What we couldn't finish, my superstitious companions left on altars in sacred groves, or at the foot of twisted trees.

From my travel mates I discovered how innocent and circumscribed my life had been, and how much more there was to learn about the depravity of man. Though they traveled as representatives of the Pope, and considered themselves men of the cloth, they stopped to pay their respects at every brothel along the way. Among their conquests were nuns selling their flesh to support their passage to Rome. The nuns were not beyond reproach, for if they had been living innocent, God-fearing lives at home, they would not have needed to travel to Rome to seek forgiveness. In Piacanza one of our shameless crew entered a nun who was bleeding. The devil entered him that night, and by morning he was dead.

On the road to Pavia we stumbled on a scene from Sodom: a huge drunken bull of a man copulating with a ewe. My drunken companions, roaring with delight, jumped from their wagons and ran to help him. The phrase "lost sheep" took on new meaning.

I had nothing but contempt for these men, who succumbed to the flesh each night and weighed their lives in gold and silver. Their harsh laughter grated on me. Their beards smelled of congealed grease. And yet their voices comforted me at night-fall, when the spirits of the dead came to disturb us, and devils danced around enchanted springs.

IT WAS A FEAST DAY WHEN WE PULLED INTO PAVIA, SO we drove straight to the fair. Tents were raised on a flat grassy field inside the monastery walls. Flaps opened and closed like bird wings. A line of wooden crosses held monks back from tempta-tion. Having no such restraints, I bought sword buckles, filigreed cross-belts, hairpins, earrings—anything I could sell or trade for food along the way. The Frankish pound was heavier than ours, so I stocked up on gold, both Moslem dinar and Byzantine *nom-isma*. If that was a fair exchange rate, the earth is round.

A hogshead of sifted flour set me back eight denier. I ran my fingers across an otter's cloak on sale for 360 denier, the cost of five healthy oxen. Who but a king or pope, I wondered, could afford such luxury?

As we left town, we passed a blacksmith hammering a strip of soft iron into a longsword under a shower of sparks. His body glistened. His face was furnace-red. A blind beggar squatted in the dust nearby, listening for the clink of coins in his wooden bowl. I gave him some change and asked him to pray for me.

FROM AOSTA WE AVOIDED THE MOST TREACHEROUS pass, preferring the slightly longer but safer route to the west, dropping down to Lake Geneva. As we headed up into the mountains, we haggled with some fierce-looking Marrones from

St. Tropez, who demanded an inheritance to bring us and our baggage across the pass. We had no choice. We could part with our silver or our lives.

We climbed slowly into a blind, mineral world, seasonless, where nothing seemed to bloom or fade. Snow whirled about us like woodland sprites. Our beards stiffened, our ink bottles filled with ice. I had to jump from my wagon and walk along beside it to keep from freezing. Our guides wore boots with iron points, and punched the snow with staves.

When the wind howled, I chanted mass or sucked the sweetness from my white Syrian pistachios. I popped the slightly open shells into my mouth and pushed them into my cheeks and rolled them around my tongue, licking the bony ridges and drawing the taste of the East from them. I either devoured my daily allotment in a few moments of self-indulgence, or I rationed it into many small, deliberate pleasures and spread them through the day. Whether I gorged myself or took my time, finishing the last one filled me with an inexplicable sadness. Then I would suck on an empty shell until my tongue tasted of blood.

The descent into Gaul was more gradual, but just as treacherous. We hung to the guides. Once we lay on our backs and crawled along like crabs. We bound our horses' legs and slid them down a mountain on ox hides. A cart broke loose and shattered against some ancient oaks.

GAUL WAS A LAND OF MARSHES AND SWAMPS, DENSE forests and sudden clearings.

Coming upon a settlement gave my spirits a great lift after days in the woods. What an affirmation there was in the heady smell of fresh manure, the sight of wood smoke curling up through the trees, smudging the air. There were never more than a few houses, huddled together in a clearing, but when we broke out of the forest I felt I was back in God's world, safe from wild beasts and the hooting of owls and demons. It was as close to a homecoming as I had ever known.

FIFTEEN

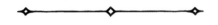

· 811 AD ·

I T WAS A BRISK, EARLY SPRING EVENING WHEN I MET GODEL. THE WORLD WAS BURSTING WITH LIFE. WE RODE PAST SOME STARTLED SHEEP AND A HAND-ful of fruit trees with their small perfect leaves—medlar, plum, the sometimes sour, never sweet Gozmaringa apple. We didn't want to request more hospitality than we would receive, so my companions and I split up and went to separate homes. The one I chose had a thatched roof that came down almost to the ground: a big hat on a small head.

The kitchen garden gave off a smell of manure so strong you could have grown flowers in it. Godel was squatting in her garden among her fava beans and vetches. When she saw me, her face filled with terror. She relaxed only when I told her that I was an emissary of the Pope, looking for a dry floor to sleep on, and a home-cooked meal.

She motioned me in. Her words were a garble of Latin, German, and French, which I tied together with only limited success. Her world was an intensely local place. The room she occupied was dark and smoky. A small boy was picking at the packed earth floor with a broken stick. I squeezed myself down on a narrow bench around a rough oak table. Godel began preparing supper. She had a pretty face with a strong mouth and pinched eyes that focused on what she was doing. Her skin was lighter than mine. Whenever she raised her arm I could see her small white breasts through the opening in her sleeve. God forgive me, I never turned away.

The hut was no more than a single room supported by four corner beams. The walls were made of wooden lathes woven together and daubed with mud. One side of the hut was covered with straw. That was where the animals lived. The other side was partitioned off as a living area, with a bed, a table, an old chest and a simple wooden cradle. A strip of iron hung from the wall to ward off the devil.

"The boy's sick," Godel said. "He'll probably die."

I studied the child. His left eye was red and caked with pus, but he didn't seem to mind.

"He got sick the day the moon entered its fourth quarter," Godel said.

I nodded sympathetically and got down on all fours in front of the child, pretending to be a wild beast. I growled and rolled my head. The boy fled in terror.

"I tried putting him on the roof," Godel said, brushing the

hair from his soft face. "That didn't work, so I gave him worm-wood. He's in God's hand now."

"You may want to mix some ale with garlic and cow manure and feed it to him with the Eucharist," I said.

"A priest comes to us once a month when he's sober enough to remember," Godel said. "But it's their salvation up at the manor house he's paid to look after, not mine."

I nodded sympathetically and told her about a priest I knew in Rome who baptized children *in nomine patria et filia*, in the name of the nation and the daughter. Godel didn't smile. She didn't know a word of Latin.

"I'd rather have a bad priest than none at all," she said. "How else can we celebrate Mass?"

THIS WAS NOT IMPERIAL ROME. WE SAT UPRIGHT AT THE table and ate with our fingers from a cup. It was a meal to forget: a mash of beans and panicgrass, seasoned with cheap oil. The mulberry wine relaxed us, though, and as darkness fell we opened up to each other like night-blooming flowers and permitted ourselves an intimacy that would have been impossible among friends.

The boy wasn't Godel's, he belonged to her sister. The girl had died giving birth, and her husband had left the baby with Godel and gone to fight for Charles in Spain. Godel wanted me to know that she had never wanted to marry, but she had a farm now, and a baby to care for, so when a widower named Theodulf asked to post the banns, she had consented. He had a slit nose and was rumored to have cut his first wife in pieces and fed her to the pigs, but he was good at hauling wood and crushing molehills.

Godel swept some crumbs into her small, weathered hand and tossed them into the fire. A small flame flared and died. Godel poured more wine.

"The day he moved in, everything changed," she said. "Our hens stopped laying eggs. Our cow's milk turned sour. Theodulf had to work several months a year at the manor house, cutting firewood to make ends meet. Last fall was a disaster. We had to sell everything. Theodulf went off with his loaf of rye one morning and never came back."

The boy squatted. Godel picked him up and whirled him out the door. Too late. A chicken waddled over and pecked at the trail of brown liquid staining the floor.

"I must have given him too much fennel," Godel said guiltily. She put the boy down beside the fire. A wet log crackled. The boy jumped back, then crawled toward the flames. Godel patted his head. I belched. Godel beamed.

I tried to tell Godel about Emperor Charles, but her child was sick or dying—that was the world she lived in. It was early spring, and she had been working in the fields since dawn. While I spoke about my trip to Aachen, she curled up near the fire, rested her head on her hands, and went to sleep. The boy crawled over and pressed up against her. The fire crackled but neither stirred.

I covered them with sheepskins and then I lay down on the bed and covered myself too. The night was clear and cold. A crescent moon sat on some black branches outside my window. The wind blew. The moon rose. I glanced up at the icon on the wall and fell into a dreamless sleep.

When I awoke it was still dark but Godel was gone. I found her outside, drawing furrows around her property, hoping to discourage witches. The boy clung to her back. I made music for him through a blade of grass. He smiled. I carried him on my shoulders. I loved the way his head smelled, like goat milk, and his perfect hands and feet.

The day rose gradually out of the darkness. Godel walked beside me. Our shadows crossed. She stepped quickly aside. I asked if I could stay a few more days: a wagon wheel needed to be tightened and the new moon made it an inauspicious time to travel. She agreed but asked if my companions and I could help with the spring planting. It was seed time, the busiest time of year, she said, and most of the men and boys were away working on the lord's estate to pay their rent.

NONE OF US NEEDED CONVINCING. WE WERE ALL HAPPY to break the journey and sleep in beds. And so we joined the women and children in the fields. Virgil would have been proud of me, tracing furrows with a simple plank of wood and crushing the clods with a wooden hoe. There was no ox or plough. It was the Year of Our Lord 811, but the Franks still used the old two-plough system, burning the stubble, abandoning it for two or three years, and then starting again. It was primitive, backbreaking work, but it was satisfying work. I liked splitting the earth open with my own two hands. I felt useful. There was a sense of necessity to it, of purpose, like the sun's trip across the sky. Virgil was right, I thought. The glory of Rome is not in her soldiers but in her farmers. The bread Christ transformed into the living flesh began with them.

When I returned to Godel's home the boy was screaming. I held him while Godel grabbed a knife and pressed it to the boy's flesh. "Worm, out from the marrow of the bone," she cried. "From the bone into the flesh, from the flesh into the skin, from the skin into the knife. So be it, Lord."

She crossed herself. The late afternoon sun poured through the window. She covered it with a square of heavy cloth to keep the dust motes out. Then she prepared supper, a gruel of barley and oats thinned with oil. It was too early in the season for vegetables, so we stuffed ourselves with berries. I farted loud enough to blow the house away. Godel giggled and boiled me some apple juice with honey and pepper. I laughed at her magic brew but it did the trick. I wasn't embarrassed, that was the wonderful part. Everything was natural with Godel. I was not myself with her, I was better. I wanted to tell her that her eyes were doves but I knew she would laugh at me. I wanted to reach out and touch her white neck but I could just as easily have touched the moon.

IT WAS MY TURN TO SLEEP BY THE FIRE. I LAY DOWN BY the crackling logs and thought, "Having sex without sin is like being in a fire without burning."

Sleep was out of the question, so I unpacked a penitential I had brought with me to sell in Aachen, and crawled close to the flames. Who would have thought there were so many ways to sin: oral intercourse, anal intercourse, dorsal intercourse, fornicating with sheep, horses, goats—the list went on and on.

When at last I fell asleep, I was besieged by succubi, their faces like glowing irons, who performed wonderful, abominable acts with me. Devils disguised as moles and mice roused me through the night.

When I awoke, Godel was gone again. The fire was dead. I lay on my back and cradled my head in my hands. Birds were singing in the eaves. Leaves rustled. A stream gurgled. It was so close, it seemed to flow right through me.

When I caught up with Godel, the sun had burned the stiffness from the day. She was leaning on her hoe, looking out past the charred fields, past this vale of sorrow, at the life to come.

She slaughtered a chicken for me that last night and served it with a powerful plum wine. We danced around the table. Our lips were shiny with grease. When the boy fell asleep, Godel put him in his cradle and lay down beside the fire with me. I kissed her neck and mouth. I would have to fast for seven days, without meat or wine, but I kissed her again, with the pollution of an embrace. Then I thought of Pluto dragging Proserpine down to the underworld, and turned and said goodnight.

. . .

GODEL WAS UP LONG BEFORE ME, BAKING BREAD FOR my journey. It rose perfectly. She beamed like a child. I tossed a log on the fire. It flamed up quickly but gave off almost no heat.

"It's alder," Godel said, "the tree of misfortune."

After packing my cart, we took a last walk through the fields. Our shadows crossed. Neither of us moved. "You're the Rose of Sharon," I said. "You're a Lily of the Valley." Her face beamed. She turned away. I stared down at the grass and told her what I had told no one before, that I was an abandoned child left at the doorstep of a church.

"Rome was founded by two abandoned children," Godel said. "Our Lord Himself was abandoned twice—once by God, Who sent His Son down from Heaven to save us, and once by us, who crucified Him and let Him bleed to death on the cross."

I was silent. I could think of nothing to say. Godel grabbed my arm. "Shhh!" she said. "Look." She pointed to a bee in a briar bush. "Quick. Make a wish."

I wished I could stay forever, but it was time to go. God had other plans for me. I gave Godel the cloth that was sanctified by Peter and Marcellinus—the one I slept with every night. She gave me a sheepskin blanket, a wonderful gift. I still have it today, though I'm ashamed to be seen in something so ragged, and keep it locked away in a chest.

I picked up the boy and tried to hug him, but he wriggled free and grabbed Godel. I was too choked up to speak. The Pope's men were waiting. I climbed into my wagon. We jolted forward. The forest closed around us.

As we bumped along, I tried to conjure up Godel's face. It was gone. Godel, the farm, the clearing in the woods—all belonged to another life. Yet even today, when I walk through the catacomb of Peter and Marcellinus, I look up at the painting of the humble family sitting down to dinner, and think of Godel and her child. *Misce me,* mix the wine for me, I tell the servants. *Da calda.* Make it warm.

SIXTEEN

◆───────◆───────◆

W E WERE WEAVING THROUGH A GREAT
BROODING FOREST OF MAPLES AND OAKS,
BORDERED BY SWAMPS AND BOGS, WHEN
a huge brass eagle suddenly appeared through the branches,
poised for flight. Charles's palace was just ahead. How amazing, I thought, the ruler of the world, the new David, living in
this wilderness.

Birds sang their own version of Matins as we rode past the
barns and sheepfolds, the cabins of tenants and serfs. The great
May Fair was beginning. We splashed through excrement from
every corner of the kingdom.

My companions were led off to a hostel, without a backward glance. I was relieved to be free of them, but for a moment
I felt bereft.

A stooped, gnarled excuse of a man stepped forward and
demanded my treasure. Hunchbacks are banned from heaven,

but not, apparently, from Aachen. He lifted my chest of bones like a wheel of cheese, and swung it into his cart. It must have weighed more than he did.

The royal palace rose before me. I imagined myself climbing the monumental stairway to the great reception hall, and kneeling before the emperor with my treasure. But I was a little man on a big stage. My work was done. I could climb into my wagon and head home. No one would know. No one would care.

The little man led me past a statue of the barbarian king Theodoric, forever charging across the lawn on his brass steed, and deposited me at a gap in a low stone wall. This was the entrance to Charles's famous baths. It was a startling sight. Dozens of bodies floated in the steaming air, as naked as the day they were born. Children firm and shiny as winter berries splashed about in the stinking, sulfurous waters, screaming with delight. Young men, hairy as beasts, filled their cups with water flowing from a long thin pipe, and sipped it like wine. Old men waded by, wrapped in skin as wrinkled as Syrian plums. Who was who? Without clothes, it was impossible to tell.

A man with a large round head and bulging eyes told me to peel off my stinking clothes and jump in. I didn't need to be told twice, and sank into the healing waters. The warmth swaddled me. People were laughing, debating, singing godless Germanic songs that made me blush. Three months of fear and loneliness began to fall away. I had heard that Charles made his home at Aachen, not to be near God but to soak in these steaming baths. For a moment I could almost forgive him.

When the man with the bulging eyes stood to leave, I could see that he was very short, but well-endowed. I watched him walk away, strutting like a cock.

I strained to hear two men discussing the symbolism of Solomon's sixty wives and eight hundred concubines.

"I should be so lucky...," "abomination...," "dog in heat..."

All I could hear were German phrases.

Two middle-aged men shared a lewd joke about a flea with gout. A group of glistening schoolboys stood around their teacher, practicing their lessons. He towered over them.

"Tell me," he said. "What is Man?" His voice was very high. It could have been a girl's.

Several voices rang out together.

"The bondsman of death."

"A passing wayfarer."

"A guest sojourning on Earth."

I recognized these as the dialogues of Alcuin, the English cleric who dominated Charles's court. They were required reading for every Frankish schoolboy. Anyone who expected to advance in his career could recite them in his sleep.

"Now, to what is man like?" the teacher continued.

"To an apple on a tree," the boys shot back.

The teacher turned to a very slim, fair-skinned boy, and placed a huge hand on his spindly shoulder.

"And how is he placed?"

The boy cringed. A look of terror brushed his face.

"Man. How is he placed?"

The boy froze like a cornered animal. The teacher slapped him. I heard the sound of the *primicerius* kissing me, and turned away.

"Like a lantern in the wind," the teacher whined. Then, without a further word, he turned and waded off into the waters.

It was Charles.

The teacher was Charles, king of the Franks, emperor of the world. Twelve years had taken their toll on him. His flesh drooped from his waist in bunches. His right arm hung uselessly by his side. When I looked closely at him I could see his skull staring out at me from behind his wrinkled face.

One should never see an emperor in a bath, I thought. But it was not the aging or the nakedness that upset me, it was the sound of Charles's hand slapping a young boy. I had come to Aachen to worship the second Constantine, but all I saw was a fading Germanic chieftain whose ancestors lived in caves.

THE EMPEROR ROSE FROM THE WATER LIKE A WOUNDED leviathan and lowered himself into a chair. His attendants wrapped him in a loose linen shirt and a blue tunic reaching down to his feet. Lifting his massive legs, they pulled up his cross-gartered hose and laced his boots. He pushed himself to his feet and extended his heavy arms so that his attendants could wrap a sword belt around his waist. The scabbard was empty.

"I'll have roast venison today," Charles said. "And if the title Augustus means anything, you'll serve it just off the spit."

Someone—Charles's physician, perhaps—raised a hand in protest. "It's Friday," he said. "On Friday you have cream cheese."

"Cream cheese will be the death of me," Charles grumbled. "Bring me my Augustine."

The emperor grabbed the *Confessions* from a servant and lumbered off toward the palace. He was followed by his hangers-on, wagging their tongues, hoping, no doubt, for a slice of Episcopal property and other preferments.

"You're the first dialectician of the world," one of them said.

"Your mind is broader than the Nile," said another.

I STROLLED OVER TO THE FAIRGROUNDS. TENTS WERE rising through a sea of crates and cartons, overflowing with goods from every corner of the world. The little man from the baths was here, bargaining for figs. I indulged in a bag of pistachios.

Jewish merchants scurried from tent to tent, buying and selling in a Babel of tongues. There were no strangers among them. A Radonite Jew named Isaac invited me to join him for a cup of tea. He had a scarred face with furry eyebrows, watery lips, and a sharp thin nose—the trademarks of his race. A clump of black hair grew from a mole in his left cheek. He liked to twirl it around his second finger, and then twirl it again.

He turned to me.

"A dozen Croats," he said. "Can you believe it? That's what the Court wants from me for the privilege of trafficking in flesh. It's extortion. The Children of Darkness can travel freely around the kingdom, but the emperor exacts a heavy price for his beneficence."

Isaac poured the tea. It was smooth as silk and tasted of the East.

"I trade in people," he said, wasting no time. "You're a Christian, no? You could work for me on the Sabbath."

He allowed himself a grin.

"You're not a Jew," he continued, twirling his face hair. "You're blessed. What other faith would make you circumcise your slaves and then forbid you from selling circumcised slaves to Christians? You could do that for me, no?"

He told me that if I agreed to work for him, he would give me an apartment in Mainz, at the crossroads of the northern trading routes. He also promised to let me travel. Bari, Naples, Marseilles, Alexandria, Baghdad, Medinah—the names rolled off his tongue like jewels.

I pressed him for details of the slave trade.

"We trade in prisoners, not slaves," he said, popping a filbert in his mouth. "We round them up after each of Charles's campaigns, and bring them to Mainz to fatten them up. Trust me, it's in our interest to treat them well. Then we march them down the coast—Avars, Bulgars, Slavs, whatever God or fortune give us—and trade them for whatever we can make a profit on back home—camphor, cinnamon, cloves, whatever."

"I hear you take away their sex."

Isaac slapped the table. "Neuter them, you mean? The Torah forbids it. We are not butchers. I can't even slaughter an ox myself, I have to buy it from a Christian. A Jew who mutilates a man must set him free."

ISAAC'S OFFER WAS TEMPTING. THERE WAS NOTHING keeping me in Aachen. I had delivered the relics and seen enough of Charles. I could head home tomorrow if I chose, but I was in no rush to return to a city of foreigners who cared nothing for Rome's ancient glory and kept me up all night with their curses and cries.

The world Isaac held out for me was a child's world—a place of bright colors and exotic smells that had intoxicated me as a youth, wandering through Rome's central marketplace. I missed Peter and Marcellinus, and their home in the safe, silent corridors of the dead, but I wasn't ready to turn my back on the living.

God wouldn't mind my working for Isaac, I was sure. He wouldn't have brought us together if He did. Besides, slaves were not God's children. Leviticus tells us we may buy them and treat them as our property, so long as we treat them well.

"Some of us were put on earth to be slaves, others to be free," Isaac said.

"Let me think it over," I replied.

"Take all the time you need," he said. "I'm not leaving until tomorrow."

I WALKED OVER TO CHARLES'S CHAPEL, EAGER FOR GUID-ance. The Pilgrim Mass was about to begin. I looked up and saw my chest of relics balanced on a window ledge, warding off spirits that come from the west. The chapel itself was not a Roman basilica but a polygon with a huge octagonal dome—a crude version of Rome's Saint Vitale, with a muscular strength that made me cringe. The doorway was shaped like a triumphal arch, more the entrance to a royal city than to a house of God.

Emissaries from every corner of the world milled about, conversing in a multitude of tongues. Belgian chieftains exchanged toothless grins with Arab emirs. Landowners from Aquitaine grumbled about the size of their annual donations of gold and cheese. Poets, abbots, legionnaires; Irishmen, Spaniards, French—we mingled freely.

The huge brass doors finally groaned open, and I passed through the gaping entranceway into the rounded belly of the church. As I reached the inner sanctum, my eyes leaped up to the great dome where Christ our King stood enthroned in a golden, star-filled heaven. His hands were raised in blessing. This was no shepherd with his staff, it was the Lord of Creation, distant, severe, the Commander of the Troops. The twenty-four elders of the Apocalypse rose around Him, thanking Him for reigning and judging the dead. Every arch, every wall was covered with paintings and mosaics. This was not a church. It was a chieftains' trophy room, sumptuous and dazzling.

Morning light streamed through the windows and pooled on the altar. The incense made my head reel. An organ rumbled. I was shocked by this pagan intrusion in a House of God. Where were the Roman chants, the pure, bell-like sounds of young boys at plainsong?

There was a commotion in the upper gallery. We craned our necks upward like baby birds asking to be fed. It was Charles, approaching his throne with heavy steps.

"He only is my rock and my salvation," the priest intoned.

An altar boy swatted a fly with an ivory flabellum.

"He is my defense. I shall not be moved."

The priest rolled the words around on his tongue and spoke with a restlessness, a passionate estheticism, unknown to us in Rome. He bowed and genuflected. He kissed the altar, the Gospel book, the paten. I shuddered to think what God would make of a service so theatrical and unrehearsed. The silences were agonizing. I shifted my weight from one foot to the other.

AS SOON AS THE SERVICE ENDED, I RUSHED TO THE DOOR. It was a blessing to be back in the sun, bathed in God's light. I had had enough of Aachen. I had dreamed of finding a second Rome, a new Jerusalem, but all I could see was a glorified country estate ruled by a rheumatic old man surrounded by dependents, promoters, concubines, and bastard children with names like Richbod, Theodrade, and Rothilde. There was no empire, only an aging Frankish king with his personal patrimony, dwindling by the day. There was no Roman law. Charles was the law. There was no Roman administration. Charles was the administration. None of this would survive him—not for long.

THE HAMMERING IN THE MINT REMINDED ME HOW LITtle silver I had, and how rich I might become if I went to work for Isaac. I was too self-absorbed to remember God's admonition, "Vanity of vanities. All is vanity."

I passed back through the gates and into the fairgrounds. As I crossed the Jewish quarter, I wondered how the blood of ancient Rome could be so polluted, while the blood of an exiled people remained so pure; how an empire that once ruled the world could lose its way, while a people doomed to wander the earth always seemed to know where they were going.

Isaac was expecting me. He invited me in.

Alcuin was right, I thought. We are all passing wayfarers, bondsmen of death. But whoever follows in God's path shall have eternal life.

SEVENTEEN

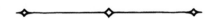

· 812 AD ·

A FEW WEEKS LATER I WAS LIVING IN A DAMP, WINDOWLESS ROOM IN MAINZ. ISAAC INSISTED THAT I LEARN THE TRICKS OF THE TRADE before I ventured out on the road, so he gave me a few days' training in the art of preparing female slaves for the auction block. I was aroused and disgusted by the rank, gamey smell of female flesh—the stink of mortality—and I soaked for hours in the public baths each afternoon, trying to wash it off.

Before long I was turning dark-haired girls into blondes, removing unseemly face hair, and making straight hair curly. I hid small scars and pimples, and masked evil odors with pleasant scents, which could almost double a slave's worth. Isaac gave me a few extra coins for each girl who could carry a tune.

Baghdad paid a bounty for them. All the professional female singers there were slaves.

I make no apologies for my work. I gave girls from backward races a more flattering appearance, and brought them within the pale of civilization. If a girl had bad teeth, I polished them with potash and sugar until they glistened. I colored fingertips of white girls red, imitating nature, which works with opposites. Who is to say that one of the slaves I prepared for market hasn't become the wealthy steward of a nobleman, guarding treasures greater than I'll ever know? Given her freedom, she may pass through the gates of heaven one day, and walk beside me in the Garden.

ISAAC WAS IN NO RUSH TO LET ME TRAVEL, SO I CON-tinued to perfect my skills, using my free time to learn about his business.

Traffic was brisk in young, light-skinned Bulgar girls under nine, but we could hardly give the older, darker ones away. Dancing and beasting was all they were good for. Their teeth were white, thanks to an excess of saliva, but their armpits smelled like the gates of hell, and nothing I did could improve their nature.

Croat girls went fast because they were good breeders, and when they divorced they became virgins again. Croat men were good at handicrafts, but many of them languished away from home and died of apoplexy. Armenian women were in demand because they were well-built and light-colored, but they had ugly feet and chastity was unknown to them.

The true aristocrats of slaves, the ones God chose for

servitude, were the Slavs. I lavished attention on them. They were cheerful and adaptable. A decent-looking but untrained Slav girl went for twice the cost of a Turk.

WHEN ISAAC SWORE THAT JEWS NEVER CASTRATE slaves, he must have meant they hired others to do it for them. I found this out one morning when I was instructed to touch a young boy's testicles after his operation. It had to be done, Isaac explained, because sometimes a slave is so frightened during the procedure that one of his stones flies up into his body, and stays there until after the incision has cicatrized. If I could feel the stone on the right side, it meant the boy could recover his semen and his passion. If I could feel the one on the left, it meant he could also grow a beard. I was relieved when I felt nothing. It meant the operation was a success.

I LAY IN A STEAMING BATH ONE AFTERNOON, THINKING grimly that my mother hadn't sacrificed her life so that her son could fondle the testicles of eunuchs. The Psalmist tells us that joy always follows a night of weeping, but all I saw were tears.

The moans and screams began each night at midnight, as I lay tossing on my damp bed. Unable to sleep, I followed the unholy sounds to an open doorway and stepped inside. I felt faint, but a voice told me to gather my courage and not be afraid. Lanterns flickered on the walls, as they do in church. A boy, pale and pasty as a ghost, lay naked on a wide wooden plank. His chest heaved. A young man bent over him with a knife. I stepped closer.

The boy howled in agony as the knife cut through his scrotum. I crossed myself but refused to turn away. The boy went limp. The man wiped his knife on a blood-stained cloth. He looked familiar. I searched the past.

Luniso?

Could it really be him, my fearless classmate, the boy who led me blindly through the catacombs? When we last met we were children playing hide-and-seek on the Palatine.

"Luniso, is it you?" I whispered.

"Who's there?"

"Deusdona."

His face glowed in the light.

"Deusdona," I repeated. "From the Schola Cantorum."

He turned toward me with a glimmer of recognition.

"Is he dead?" I asked, pointing to the boy.

Luniso chuckled. His teeth were rotting. "He'll be ready for the auction block next week," he said.

"What unpleasant business."

Luniso's mind was elsewhere. "Do you know what Caliph Amen calls his eunuchs?" he asked. "The white ones are grass-hoppers. The black ones are ravens." He broke into laughter, as though he had never heard anything so funny. It was the laughter of the lost, of those whom God has abandoned.

An assistant finally took over and Luniso was free to leave. He voiced no objection when I followed him through the damp, dim, early-morning streets to his apartment. He spoke fitfully. I struggled to put his words together.

It seemed that he had been amusing himself at the slave market near the Forum one afternoon when a Jew named Isaac offered him a cup of jasmine tea and a job helping to revitalize a sluggish slave trade among the Avars. Luniso had accepted. I wasn't surprised. It was just like him, plunging into a new life without a moment's reflection. He was returning from a slave-gathering mission six months later when his horse, frightened by a snake, bolted and sent him flying into a bed of thorns. His body recovered, but not his mind. His hands were steady, though, and one of Isaac's workers, a Christian, taught him the art of castration.

"Isaac told me Jews can't do that," I said.

"I'm not a Jew," Luniso reminded me.

When we parted, my old classmate lurched forward and wrapped me in his arms. I stood still, waiting for him to finish. "The end is near," he announced. Then he grinned and stepped inside. "I'm leaving tomorrow and don't know when I'll be back," he said.

I never saw him again.

· 813 AD ·

KING CHARLES WAS ALREADY INTERRED NEAR HIS CHAPEL when I learned of his death. It was said that the moment he left us, the sun dropped below the earth and the eagle above his palace was struck with lightening and crashed to the ground.

News followed days later that Charles's only surviving son, Louis, was on his way from Aquitaine to claim the throne. He couldn't come soon enough. Men with wealth or influence were picking away at Charles's inheritance, like crows. The empire was in tatters. Mainz was filled with deserters from Charles's army. Dispossessed farmers clogged the streets, begging for bread. The slave trade had slowed to a crawl; I could have made a better living selling horses, which feed themselves. The words of Jeremiah rang in my ears: "That which I have built will I break down, and that which I have planted I will pluck up, even this whole land."

The moaning continued, night after night. I was restless and ready to travel, but Isaac had no intention of letting me leave. I missed Peter and Marcellinus beyond words. They were my family. They were my only friends. I missed the Eternal City—afternoons in the public baths, Virgil in the Forum, a market-place bursting with colors and tastes, the ring of church bells, centering me, calling me home. Rome was only a shadow of her old self, but God, leading an army of saints and martyrs, would sweep out the barbarians, give us back our inheritance, and make us great again.

Isaac couldn't believe that I'd run off and desert him. "I put time and money in you," he sighed. "We had an agreement. This is not how Jews treat Jews."

"I inconvenienced you," I acknowledged.

"Betrayed me," he said.

He sighed deeply, and in his sigh I could hear the sorrow of his race.

"I can set you up with some Jewish traders leaving for Rome tomorrow," he said, wanting me to know he held no grudges.

"I'll arrange everything. They'll treat you well." He twirled some black face hairs around a finger. "The penalty for killing a Jew is ten pounds of gold," he grinned. "Stick with the Children of Darkness and you'll be safe."

I thanked him and bought my way into a group of Radonite Jews heading south. Ninety days later I was back in Rome.

EIGHTEEN

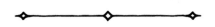

· 814 AD ·

CHOKED WITH EMOTION, I HITCHED ROMULUS TO A PLANE TREE ALONG THE VIA LABICANA AND SCRAMBLED DOWN INTO THE CHAPEL OF my beloved friends Peter and Marcellinus. I had been away more than four seasons, and the altar was thick with dust and crawling with rodents. Graffiti defiled the walls. The tomb itself, though, had not been violated. God had kept an eye on His martyrs in my absence. I dropped to my knees and wept. I was home at last. No one slapped children here. No one moaned in the night.

I stopped by my room only long enough to drop off my belongings and satisfy myself that nothing had been stolen or tampered with. God had been watching over me, too.

Then I went off to reacquaint myself with Rome.

The city belonged, more than ever, to foreigners. There were Franks everywhere—people with names that ended in -old, -bald, -rich, and -brand. You had to be a Jew to understand the babble in the marketplace. Streets were flooded with Syrians, Frisians, Lombards, Greeks. A flock of Anglo-Saxon nuns went fluttering by.

A dark-skinned couple from North Africa now occupied the room below me, and ran the tiny green grocery store that opened on to the street. The two of them eked out a living selling overripe vetches and fruits that stunk up the building. When I first met the man, Sergius, he was wearing a tunic stained with oil and fish paste. Just looking at him made me want to wash. I called him Saint Sergius. He laughed and took it as a compliment. When I passed his wife, she turned away, as though I were diseased. I still don't know her name. I suppose I could have asked.

The new Rome belonged to shopkeepers like Saint Sergius, who thought nothing of throwing spoiled fruit out their windows late at night, or dumping trash in stairwells, attracting rats and flies. The city was also a breeding ground for men of the cloth like Pope Leo—sycophants with their gaudy and extravagant ways, who tried to substitute this world for the next. When I stepped inside the Pope's new basilica, the shiny mosaics and bright, gold-embroidered fabrics outshone the small, steady flame of faith that burned in my heart, ensnaring me in this world on my way to the next. I couldn't imagine praying in the Pope's presence. When I sought forgiveness or inner strength, I climbed down into the chapel of the blessed saints Peter and Marcellinus.

I found peace there, and coolness in the heat of day. The Christ portrayed on the walls was not the distant warrior king I had seen on the dome of Charles's chapel at Aachen. He was a shepherd leading his flocks through green pastures. When he played his lyre, I could hear the music of the spheres.

TO BRING LIGHT TO A DARK WORLD, AND TO MAKE A LIV-ing, I went back to my old job, sweeping dust from the holy tombs into tiny cloth bags and selling them to pilgrims. I also sold strips of sanctified cloth and vials of holy oil—the usual.

· 816 AD ·

IN THE SPRING OF THE TWENTY-FIRST YEAR OF HIS EPIS-copate, the pope passed on. God must have had enough of his servant's dissolute ways. Standing before his Maker, Leo must have hoped God would treat him better than the furious mob who long ago dragged him from his horse and left him lying half-dead in a pool of blood. Once again, his eyes must have filled with terror.

Our next pope was Stephen, a former deacon who brought peace to the city for the few months that he was with us. Everyone loved him. He had the wise, refined, contemplative features you would expect of someone born into an old, aristocratic Roman family. I prayed that my dream of a single empire under God— the promise of Charles's coronation—would at last come true. But a few months later Stephen was gone. He left us on a cold January morning, shortly after an unnatural cluster of comets appeared in the sign of Sagittarius.

· 817 AD ·

GOD GAVE US POPE PASCHAL ON A DRAB WINTER DAY. HE had a stern, slightly scowling face and a long, scrawny beard like the tail of a raccoon. Raise your eyes above the altar at Saint Prassede and you'll see the Pontiff's long, vain, over-refined face staring contemptuously down on you.

No sooner was Paschal sworn in than he began gathering Rome's neglected martyrs, more than twenty-five hundred of them, and burying them within the city walls. As deacon of the Third Cemeterial District, a position of consequence, I was charged with identifying and labeling the saints and martyrs, and overseeing the clergy as they wrapped the relics in hand-sewn pillows, laid them in wagons, and brought them solemnly and ceremoniously to their new home in Saint Peter's. I was terrified that the saints would punish me for disturbing their sleep, but weeks passed without incident, and I took for truth what I still believe today, that the saints and martyrs, long neglected, were grateful to be safe and cared for.

You can imagine my outrage when Paschal, nourished by the Prince of Darkness, began selling off our sacred protectors to the Franks, enraging God, who punished us with high winds, fierce rains, and floods. Many drowned.

I swore I'd put an end to this evil, and when a papal officer ordered me to bring him the holy martyr Tibertius, I obeyed the voice of God instead, and delivered the worthless remains of a barber from the Jewish catacomb in the Villa Torlonia. To protect the true Tibertius from prying hands, I put him where the Jew had been. No one would think to look for him among the Children of Darkness.

I felt a special fondness for Tibertius. He occupied a chapel next door to Peter and Marcellinus for more than five hundred years. While they were alive, the three Christians must have shared an occasional meal and swapped stories over pitchers of warm, foamy beer. They may even have perished by the same sword. I could imagine them in neighboring chapels, whiling away the centuries, debating the news of the hour and chatting about the life to come. I swore to reunite them once I could guarantee their safety.

On my way home from the Villa Torlonia, the sky turned dark and menacing, and something sinister began nibbling away at the sun. People young and old crowded into the streets, blowing horns and throwing stones, trying to scare the darkness away. I had seen the sky grow black before. This was not the Day of Reckoning. Still, I didn't know for sure, and when the sun broke free from its prison and continued its journey across the sky, I joined in the celebration, as giddy as a child.

A few days later Paschal's notary returned, requesting Sebastian's lower jaw. I accommodated him with a jaw I had plucked from a stream on my way home from Mainz. Everyone was pleased. Paschal acquired a bone he could claim was sacred, and Rome got to keep Sebastian. When the notary asked me to favor him with the strip of holy linen that was used to wipe Saint Felicity's forehead at her martyrdom, I gave him a rag soaked in the blood of a slaughtered cock.

MY BUSINESS WAS SOLID, BUT THE TIMES DEMANDED more of me than I was able to, or cared to, give. While I stayed at home, sweating off weight in the public baths or listening to blind poets reciting Virgil at the Forum, Felix and his cronies began circulating north among the Franks, calling on monasteries and abbeys with order forms for every saint and martyr, and every bone in the body. Their trunks were crammed with samples.

While I lounged around at home, waiting for customers, our godless Pope traded priceless bones for power and influence. Unless I learned to move with greater urgency, our city's great chapels would be reduced to empty cells, the refuge of bats and ravenous dogs. Rome would have no one to defend her but shopkeepers and old men.

MY VOW TO SERVE GOD AND PROTECT HIS SAINTS AND martyrs was tested a few weeks later, when one of King Louis's messengers summoned me back to Aachen. I was instructed to deliver without delay the earthly remains of Saint Denis of Paris, known to us in Rome as Dionysius. It had to include his right leg. The king already had two left ones.

It was said that after he was decapitated, Dionysius took his head on a six-mile walk, preaching a sermon along the way. You had to love him for that. He was a cephalophore, a head carrier, a talking head. Not many Romans knew this. Or seemed to care. Whether I called him Saint Denis or Dionysius, I couldn't give him away.

I was also told to bring the left forearm of Saint Bibanus, the Merovingian bishop of Saintes. Bibanus never achieved much prominence, but who can account for the tastes of a king?

It was an opportunity I couldn't ignore. I could bring Louis all the bones he wanted, while spreading the faith among the Franks, at no cost to me or to Rome. If it pleased God, I would run into the emperor's chief advisor Einhard, who spent most of his days at the palace in Aachen, and sell him a relic or two for his new abbey church at Mulinheim. On my way back to Rome I could stop in on Abbott Hildoin at his abbey in Soissons. He had recently added the title archchaplain to his list of worldly credits, and would be thrilled to pick up any relics that came his way and pay sky-high prices for them. Particularly if Einhard coveted them, too. The two abbots were always at each other's throats. I could play them off against each other, in God's name.

AS SOON AS THE ALPINE ROADS OPENED UP, I HEADED north with a party of Venetian merchants. Armed with faith, I threw myself into the den and learned to live with the lions.

NINETEEN

◆━━━━◆━━━━◆

ANYONE WHO TELLS YOU THERE'S NOTHING NEW UNDER THE SUN HAS NEVER BEEN TO AACHEN IN THE SPRING. ON MY FIRST VISIT, long ago, Charles's palace rose from the woods like a pillar of light in a dark and dreary world. Now fields and farmsteads stretched for miles in every direction, and variegated vetches grew where devils used to hide.

On my last visit I was a moonstruck kid standing at the palace gates, hoping for a glimpse of the great Emperor Charles. Now Charles was dead, and I was a Roman deacon delivering bones to Charles's son, the Emperor Louis.

Doing God's work.

It was a Saturday when I arrived, the Jewish day of rest, and the market tents were all bound shut. A wild dog tore at a human skull in the field where Isaac and I once sipped tea together, bantering about the slave trade. Only God Himself could have arranged such an improbable meeting. Only He could have foreseen that within days I'd be in the hire of Jews, trading in Slavs and Croats.

I thought of cracking the dog's skull in pieces, aging them, and selling them as relics of John the Baptist. But the dog's growl was less than hospitable, and prudence warned me to keep my distance.

The sun turned as pale and flat as the Host—God's flesh made visible in the late afternoon sky. A boy with radiant blue eyes handed me a note from Einhard, inviting me to supper. I was thrilled. Rumor had it that Einhard was restoring his church in Mulinheim, and looking for a relic or two to sanctify it. Who could help him better than I? He was also known to serve his guests a transcendent roast chicken, and to sweeten his wine with honey from his own bees. His two estates—gifts from the Crown for years of service—were generously stocked with cows and sheep, wines and cheeses. We would eat well. I farted, just imagining the size of his larder.

RUMOR HAD IT THAT CHARLES'S PAGAN COFFIN WAS AN affront to Our Lord. Curious to find out why, I wandered over to his chapel and found him awaiting eternity in a huge solid block of marble carved in Rome in the days of Septimius Severus, long before Christ, in his goodness, came down and walked among us. How did this pagan box get here, I wondered? By what leap of faith did it make it across the Alps? It could not have survived without God's help.

A garish plaque hung from the chapel wall, touting Charles

as "the unifier of the Franks." It was an achievement befitting a barbarian king, I thought. If only he had taken the next step and united us all, Franks and Romans, into a Holy Roman Empire under God.

Suddenly my blood roared. My head grew light. Among the hideous shapes and forms carved into Charles's marble sarcophagus was the tortured face of Proserpine, swooning in Pluto's lewd embrace. His chariot raced toward Hades, pulled by four glistening horses, their ears thrown back, their muscles swollen with the joy of flight. Proserpine leaned back into him, eyes closed, lips parted, beyond language, the folds of her gown billowing in the wind. Her mother Ceres drew near, but late, too late.

I wanted to turn and run, but couldn't. Like Charles, I was drawn to the world of the flesh and could stare forever at the Lord of Darkness dragging a blameless woman down into his stinking pit.

God in His mercy finally released me from Proserpine's grip. I had had my fill of Charles, and wandered across the palace grounds, anxious to learn what Einhard wanted of me, and what his servants had prepared for dinner. Hours passed. Time hung like a millstone around my neck.

GOD BROUGHT EINHARD AND ME TOGETHER BY WILDLY divergent paths. I arrived in the world penniless; he was born to comfort. While I was splashing in donkey piss on the Palatine, he was studying Virgil and Livy at the abbey at Fulda. While I was in Mainz, handling the testicles of neutered slaves, he was in Aachen, handling the education of Lothar, the emperor's son.

When I saw the tiny man with the large head and bulging eyes, I recognized him as the well-endowed dwarf I had met in Charles's baths on my first visit to Aachen. So this was Einhard, I thought! Why had God favored such a tiny man? Why had he made so great a man so small? It seemed an abomination.

"After you," Einhard said, waving me into the great hall. With such gestures one makes friends for life.

Einhard scrambled up into a high chair, like a child. His feet dangled above the floor. The ceiling towered over us.

Six green-eyed Slavs—bounty, no doubt, from Charles's wars—stood with their backs to the walls, waiting to serve us. As the sun sank below the earth, tapers were lit. A dove flitted from lamp to lamp, trying to find his way back into God's kingdom. Wine arrived in silver goblets, sweetened with golden honey. I prefer a darker, bolder taste, but I was not about to complain. We raised our cups. "To Louis, and the kingdom of the Franks," Einhard said.

"And to the City of God," I rushed to add.

The meal began with pond frogs dressed in a mysterious green sauce made from the juice of sorrel. Frogs are known to carry the spirits of unbaptized children, so I made the sign of the cross with my legs under the table. Einhard licked the bones clean.

I couldn't keep my eyes off the little man. His face was young for someone who had survived fifty winters, but his chin sagged and his hands were creased and veiny. He tapped his thick, fleshy fingers on the table incessantly, as though he had too much energy for such a small body and couldn't contain it all. He moved with curious, jerky movements, like a squirrel.

The servants gave us each a small loaf of rye, a food more fitting for a menial than a man of God. Einhard must have known how to treat a privileged visitor from Rome—perhaps he was trying to impress me with his thrift. The bread was heavy as lead. Surely not the bread Christ ate at the Lord's Supper. I had to chew it forever.

"So, how are your living quarters?" Einhard began, breaking the silence. "Has the emperor shown you proper respect?"

"I have blankets, but no eiderdown," I admitted, trying to find the humor.

"Love not sleep, lest thou come to poverty," Einhard smiled, sententiously. "Or travel with your own bedding, as I do."

With much flapping and fluttering, the servants placed between us a platter of boned chicken breasts, seasoned with pureed pimentos. I wanted to point out that bones enhance taste, but I knew when to keep my mouth shut. The spices drew beads of sweat from my forehead and the meat was tough as crow, but I got it all down without choking, and even managed to compliment the chef on his inventiveness. A plate of long yellow beans came next, as scrawny as a priest on a ten-day fast.

Einhard cleaned his plate, sat back contentedly, and patted his ample belly. "My days are winding down," he said, thoughtfully. "Such is life."

He paused and waited for me to acknowledge his wisdom. I nodded obligingly.

"The time has come for me to leave the weight of public service to others and retire to the land of my youth," he continued. "I need to look after my own salvation and leave tomorrow to others."

I wanted to remind him that this was not the Roman ideal of public service, but I let it go.

Einhard's voice was as oily as a votary lamp. "More than a decade ago," he said, "Emperor Louis gave me the village of Mulinheim, on the banks of the Main. I love Mulinheim. Nothing ever happens there. Dogs bark. Bees hum. People live and die. The river flows along, always changing, always the same, whatever happens to us. I want to enjoy my final days there, near the village where I was born."

"A vision of earthly peace," I said, expansively. "If God ever lets me settle down, it will be with a woman named Godel in a village like Mulinheim."

I shut my eyes and saw Godel as she first appeared to me, squatting fearfully in a field of vetches.

Einhard permitted himself a smile, which I returned with genuine affection. I couldn't help it. He was full of himself, but there was honesty in his voice. I liked him, despite his size—no, because of it. It wasn't just the wine warming my heart: Behind his affectations was a man of true accomplishments and honest yearnings. How deeply I envied him, passing his final days among family and friends in Mulinheim, while I wandered the earth among the living dead.

Einhard assumed his oratorical tone again. He could have been addressing a crowd at the Forum. "My abbey church has a glorious location on high ground overlooking a bend in the river," he said. "It was a sweet, honest little place when I inherited it, but it was made of wood and better suited for owls and moles than the celebration of the Mass. Hardly what you'd call a House of God. I transformed it into a stone basilica, still modest, but worthy of Our Father, and solid enough to withstand whatever winter throws our way. All that's missing is a relic or two to sanctify the altar—the knee or foot of someone intimate with God, who will watch over our little village, cure the sick, bring us rich harvests, and improve our honey crop."

"Your saint will be busy," I quipped. Einhard wasn't amused.

"I need someone who can intercede with God for us," he said. "Someone who can ask Our Father to bring us a lead roof, so the faithful won't get rained or snowed on when they come to pray. God understands the indignity of a leaky roof. For years I've sought donations from those with means, without success. Perhaps God is punishing me for my sins, of which there are many. But I can't bear the thought of going to my final rest until my church has a proper roof."

Einhard took a sip of wine and winced with disappointment. A knife couldn't have caused more pain. A few drops dribbled down his chin. He brushed them away with the back of his stubby hand, and licked the whorls of hair growing on his knuckles.

"They tell me Hildoin bought three of Sebastian's ribs from you for an ungodly price, and displays them in their own sumptuous chapel at Saint Médard," Einhard said. "They say the line of pilgrims seeking Sebastian's blessing stretches out the front door, into the street, and that Hildoin is richer than Solomon now, if not as wise. Find me a saint of comparable appeal—someone who would be thrilled to exchange the turmoil of Rome for the tranquility of Mulinheim, and you'll make a friend for life."

I looked hard at Einhard, trying to read his heart. "At the end of the day, it's Sebastian you want," I said, cautiously. "He outperforms everyone, martyr or saint."

Einhard frowned. "The truth is," he said, "Mulinheim is too out of touch with the world, too secluded, for a luminary like Sebastian. I have a modest church with a leaky roof, a closet full of musty blankets, and a few odd beds. Sebastian is a star. He demands more. And deserves it. He told me so himself one night, curled up at the bottom of my bed. 'Country life would drive me crazy,' he said."

"Give me something to work with," I pleaded.

"Well," said Einhard, "as a starter I'd prefer a martyr to a saint. To live for God is wonderful, but to die for Him is, well, more wonderful. What Mulinheim needs are martyrs with a human touch. Men like Peter the exorcist and Marcellinus the priest. Men who lived and died together, were buried together, and will no doubt ascend to heaven together. Now there's a likeable pair worthy of a coin or two."

"Peter and Marcellinus?" I could barely speak the words.

Einhard leaned back. "You don't know them?" he asked, incredulous. "They share a single tomb, one above the other, near the via Labicana."

"I know them well," I assured him.

I hid my hands in my lap. They were sweating, and not from pimentos. As deacon of Rome's Third Cemeterial District, I was responsible for maintaining the chapel of these two celebrated martyrs. It was my second home. Peter and Marcellinus were family to me, the only family I ever had. Every week I broke bread with them around their altar. I organized their feast day every June. When I first stumbled on their tomb, it was a monument to neglect. I cleaned and restored it. I gave it the prominence and attention it deserved. Thanks to me, Peter and Marcellinus were now venerated throughout Rome. The thought of moving them made my stomach churn.

"There's something very appealing about the idea of two martyrs, a man and a boy, sharing a common tomb," Einhard said. "Don't you think? Something almost human? Pilgrims are bound to seek them out."

"There are saints better known than Peter and Marcellinus," I reminded him, with more than a hint of desperation in my voice. "Saint Cecilia, Saint Justin, Saint Polycarp…"

Einhard cut me off. "Last month Peter and Marcellinus came to me in a deep sleep and told me in no uncertain terms that they wanted to move to Mulinheim at the earliest opportunity. They take turns visiting me every morning just before dawn. See these wrinkles under my eyes? My heavenly guests won't let me sleep. I hear them groan. They won't be content until they're here with me, performing miracles, basking in my love."

"If Rome finds out, the whole city will be at our throats," I warned.

"Deusdona, you're an old hand at this. I leave it to you to find a way. If you can't help, another deacon will—a man named Felix. I expect him in a day or two."

"Felix is no deacon," I shouted. "He's a fraud. An enemy of the Church and the people."

"God works in mysterious ways," said Einhard.

I paused. Little people can be very stubborn. "Marcellinus wishes it," Einhard said. "And so does Peter. I spoke to them. They didn't mince their words."

Argument was futile. I had to promise to deliver to Einhard both martyrs, and substitute worthless bones instead. Nothing to get riled up about, really. Rome has never had a shortage of worthless bones.

More problematic was my need to waken God's most beloved saints from centuries of sleep and move them to safer quarters. In the confusion, they might think they were being molested, and punish me in unspeakable ways.

I glanced over at Einhard. "Lying lips are an abomination to the Lord," I said, solemnly. "So I must tell you I'm stopping in Saint Médard on my way home, hoping to sell Hildoin another relic or two. He never seems to have enough. Give him a hundred, he always wants a hundred more."

Einhard didn't return my smile. The rivalry between the two men ran deep. It wasn't just a numbers game. Einhard envied Hildoin his fame. Hildoin despised the little man his privileged life at Aachen, and his influence on the king. Nothing could disguise the fact that Einhard was a lay abbot who had never taken the vows, and Hildoin was an ordained priest. They butted heads like goats.

"One more thing," Einhard said. "I'm sending my notary Ratleig with you. He's a true believer, with a heart of gold. He'll bring me the holy treasure himself, before the roads freeze over. He insists. He told me so in no uncertain terms."

His business concluded, Einhard called for a platter of cheeses. I saw him raise an eyebrow when I sliced off the rind. "What in heaven's name are you doing?" he asked. "The rind is where the taste is."

I smiled derisively. Leave it to the Franks to prefer the rind to the cheese, I thought.

When we stood, I towered over him.

KING CHARLES CAME TO ME THAT NIGHT AS I THRASHED about under my scratchy blankets, a stranger to sleep. He was sitting erect in his coffin, wearing a sparkling crown, and holding a gold scepter in his gloved hand. His second finger stuck up through the glove, but he hadn't lost a single member to decay except the tip of his nose. The smell of pimentoed chicken soured the air. He said nothing. When I awoke he was gone. Birds were chirping. Spring was on its way.

I WANTED TO SET OFF IMMEDIATELY, BUT THERE WERE endless delays. I threw away a full afternoon searching for pickled barley, smoked pork—one of God's great gifts to man—and hydromel, which always brings a smile to my face. I could have saved time buying garum sauce made with smelts, but I poked around until I found a saltier version made with small mullets.

Ratleig kept us waiting while he went to pay off his debts. Einhard needed to track down a copy of the emperor's seal, guaranteeing us safe passage through his kingdom. The moon was full then, a bad omen, and we had to wait for it to wane. We were ready to go on the sixth of June but I insisted on postponing our departure until the twelfth. Twelve, we know, is a holy number, equal to the four corners of the world multiplied times the three persons of the Trinity.

THE CHAPEL ROSE DIMLY THROUGH THE SOFT, EARLY morning light as I accompanied Ratleig to the Pilgrim's Mass. Ratleig was a short, stocky man with faultless teeth. I wondered what sin, what offense to man or God, caused him to walk with a lilt. His hair was greased with rancid butter.

Ratleig couldn't wait to leave. "I plan to visit every shrine in Rome," he announced.

"That's hardly possible," I assured him. "But God is everywhere. You can reach Him through His saints."

"I want to find out why He took my three children from me," Ratleig said. "All three! None of them lived long enough to cry. None even opened his eyes. Why would God do that to them? Why would He do it to me?"

"Our father's sins are passed down to us," I tried to explain. "All our father's fathers' sins are passed down through the ages."

"My wife is having another child," Ratleig announced. "Was it wrong of me? Will God punish us again?"

"Trust in God with all thy heart and lean not on your own understanding," I told him. I wanted to reach out and touch his arm, but it would have been like touching fire. Intimacy was not my card. "That's from Proverbs," I said.

Ratleig pulled at his nose. "My wife hates my going," he acknowledged. "She's terrified she'll never see me again. But what choice do I have? The saints and martyrs are the same as everyone else. They like lilies. They like prayers and thanks. They're unhappy when they don't hear the clink of silver in their offering plates. Ask them for miracles, that's why they're there. Believe in them, pray to them, and they'll put in a good word for you with God."

"Helping the faithful, that's what saints and martyrs do," I reminded him. "Have faith. God loves those who are faithful. Miracles happen. But tell me this: Have you ever thought of asking for a daughter?"

Ratleig looked at me in disbelief. A crow flew overhead and settled on a dead tree.

WE STEPPED OUT OF GOD'S LIGHT, INTO THE DIMNESS of the chapel. The holy water was coated with a strip of ice. Candlelight flickered on Christ's face, floating in darkness, high up in the dome. The twenty-four elders were lost in shadows. I wanted to ask God to grant me a safe journey, but He seemed too far away, too absorbed in other, more weighty matters. I looked at Ratleig. His eyes were shut in silent prayer. It would be easy, I realized, to mislead a man so kind and trusting.

The morning light performed its own special alchemy on the altar, burnishing it with gold. The pilgrims inched forward one by one, lowering their heads to receive the medal of Peter and Paul. It was just a piece of hammered metal, cruder than anything I would have made or sold myself, but it would help them remember their duty to God on their long, perilous journey. I was touched by the sincerity and solemnity of the ritual.

"Receive this support for your journey, and your toil on the pilgrim road," the priest cried out, "that you may overcome all the power of the enemy, and visit safely the dwellings of the saints, and return in gladness."

There wasn't a dry eye in the chapel as the pilgrims struggled to grasp the enormity of the journey that lay ahead. I cried, too, for the first time since Charles's coronation. I was embarrassed to show my feelings so openly, but I was swept up by a sense of purpose—a holy vow to keep Peter and Marcellinus safe in Rome, free from the clutches of men like Einhard and Hildoin.

MY HORSE ROMULUS QUIVERED WITH EXCITEMENT AS I harnessed him to my wagon. He was old and tired, but he knew something was up. His back teeth were worn nearly to the bone, but he was doing what God had put him on earth to do.

Ratleig hugged his pregnant wife and climbed into the wagon beside me. I whipped Romulus hard. He snorted. The cart jolted forward. We rode out through the gate. When I looked back, the palace was gone.

TWENTY

THE FOREST PATH WAS POORLY MARKED AND FLOODED FROM SPRING RAINS. SOON WE WERE LOST. THE DAY TURNED WILD AND WINDY, SO WE stopped early. While I lit a fire and set up camp, Ratleig trapped a wild boar, cleaned it, and seasoned it with mashed peppercorns from India and dried Syrian lemons, a rare treat. The sight of Ratlieg ramming a stake through that quivering flesh made me wonder why the Christ I saw portrayed in the catacombs was always nailed to an upright post, never to a cross. Hot fat dripped from the beast like blood from Christ's wounds. Ratleig and I sat silently, almost touching, gnawing on the salty flesh. The fire crackled. Ratleig licked his shiny fingers. "The Lord's Passion," I wanted to say. But Ratleig wouldn't understand, so I put my thoughts away and cut myself another slice of meat. The pig was delicious beyond words.

DURING THE NIGHT THE WIND CALMED DOWN, THE SKY cleared, and seven lights blazed through the heavens. I stood a bottle of holy water in a corner of our tent to keep the night devils away.

THE NEXT DAY GOD RETURNED US TO THE RIGHT PATH and we continued safely on our journey, following the east bank of the Meuse south to Liege, then skirting the wild Ardennes to Soissons.

Hildoin wasn't expecting me, but I had supplied him with relics from time to time, including Sebastian. I was certain he'd be delighted to meet me and order more. Like most Franks, he was obsessed with all things Roman, particularly the remains of saints and martyrs.

HILDOIN PUT ME OFF FOR A DAY, SO I JOINED THE PIL-grims crowding into Sebastian's chapel, straining for a glimpse of the celebrated ribs. I could have been fighting for a seat in the Coliseum in the days of Vespasian. A priest tried to keep order, but we surged around him, almost knocking him down. Sebastian is known for shielding the faithful from the plague, so he is always in great demand. His offering plate overflowed with coins from every corner of the world.

Sebastian's chapel was a study in flamboyance, created for the newly converted Franks, who equated excess with good taste. In the midst of this glitter lay the sick and dying, covered with sores and pus, some stretched on litters, others swaddled in

straw blankets on the hard, cold floor. The lamentations continued without stop: "Give Thusnelda back to me...," "Let my cow
give milk...," "Give me a healthy son who can work a plow...,"
"Give us rain but not too much...."

Friends and well-wishers fed the penitents an evil-smelling
gruel of barley and oats. The stench was sickening. I was about
to flee when the priest plucked a young girl from the crowd and
carried her to the reliquary that housed Sebastian's ribs. Her knees
were so twisted, they touched her breasts. As she reached out to
kiss the holy bones, the evil spirit that possessed her fled, and she
let out an unholy scream and began shaking violently. The crowd
parted for her as she stood and walked unaided through the doorway and disappeared into the street. I lowered my head in prayer.

Ratleig and I dined alone on boiled beef and pressed curds—
an insipid meal, better suited for a doorkeeper than a deacon.
Ratleig was assigned to a dormitory. I had a small cell to myself.
The bed was covered with soft linen sheets and eiderdown. I slept
the sleep of the blessed and awoke refreshed.

HILDOIN KEPT ME WAITING IN THE FORMAL RECEPTION
hall for more than an hour. I suppose he wanted to prove his time
was worth more than mine. The chairs were tall and narrow.
"Deacon Deusdona," the abbot exclaimed, lurching toward me,
"you're a true servant of God."

He was tall and narrow, too, with a pale, undernourished
cast to his face. He leaned to the left, like a tree on a windy hill,
the mark of a hypocrite.

"Our enemies insist that Saint Sebastian is still in Rome," he said. "But he's here with us, performing miracles daily, inspiring the faithful and increasing the prestige of Saint Médard."

"Just and true are God's ways," I said.

"And that's why you're with us today," the abbot replied. "Last night Sebastian came to me in a deep sleep. He was much shorter than I imagined, with a scraggly beard."

"Were his wounds bleeding?" I asked.

"It was too dark to see. But his Latin was impeccable, and every word came through loud and clear. 'I love life at Saint Médard,' he said, 'but I'm lonely here without my friends. Can you send me some? Time crawls by without them.'

"Sebastian disappeared then, and I spent a restless night debating how to honor the saint's request. The next day God brought me you, Deusdona. The Holy Peddler. Talk about signs from Heaven."

It was a performance the devil couldn't have improved on. Stupidly, I clapped. Hildoin looked at me askance.

"I have the perfect companion for Sebastian," I said. "Tibertius."

"The Tibertius on the via Appia?"

"No, the Tibertius on the via Labicana, near the site of the two laurels. Sebastian baptized him centuries ago. Can you imagine the two of them meeting up at Saint Médard after all these years?"

"A reunion for the ages!" Hildoin said, grinning with half his face.

"It's so outrageous, only God could have thought it up," I exclaimed.

I leaned back and smiled. It was an ingenious plan. I'd give Hildoin the remains of the Jewish barber I had buried in Tibertius's grave. To the abbot, a hand was a hand, a toe a toe. He'd never know the difference.

"I think I know your Tibertius," Hildoin said. "From the martyrologies."

"His chapel is still standing, but, alas, in ruins."

"Like Rome itself," Hildoin quipped.

I allowed myself a smile.

"Tell me," Hildoin asked, "what is your Tibertius known for? Is he a patron saint? Many of our visitors today have special needs."

"As a young man, he often walked barefoot on hot coals without suffering pain or injury," I replied. "Pilgrims with sore feet still seek him out."

Hildoin smirked. His teeth were wooden, like slivers of the cross. "Sore feet are a common complaint among pilgrims, we can all agree on that," he said.

"Then you'll welcome Tibertius to Saint Médard," I cried out.

The abbott fixed me in his watery gaze. "I'm sure he'll earn his keep," he said, cracking his knuckles. "But tell me. I hear that Einhard's man Ratleig is accompanying you to Rome. I assume he'll be picking up a sacred limb or two for Einhard's church in Mulinheim. Anyone I know?"

I thought of misleading Hildoin, but there was no point. As soon as Peter and Marcellinus were safely across the Alps, Einhard would spread the word that the martyrs were headed to a new and better life in Mulinheim. When you acquire a relic, you don't hide the wonderful news, you let the world know, and you celebrate the passing days with growing joy and expectation.

The time for secrets was behind us.

"I'm sending Einhard the martyrs Peter and Marcellinus," I acknowledged. "It's Einhard's wish. The martyrs approve. They wouldn't go if they didn't."

Hildoin put on a surprised, wounded look. "Marcellinus the priest and Peter the exorcist!" he exclaimed. "The old man and the young boy. A victory, a triumph, for Einhard and his modest church."

"'God causes all things to work together,'" I said, quoting someone.

Hildoin sneered and studied his nails. They were long and sharp. "But do Peter and Marcellinus really want to waste their days in Mulinheim, entertaining spiders and mice?" he asked rhetorically. "How many pilgrims will seek them out? How many will drop coins in their offering bowl? 'Mulinheim?' they'll exclaim. 'The church with the leaky roof? I know it well. I was rained on there. Let's go to Saint Médard and stay dry.'"

Hildoin smoothed his vestments. Being bested by a rival was never an option for him. He was not one for compromise or disappointment.

A door slammed. The wind rattled the shutters. If God were trying to reach me, He was speaking in a foreign tongue.

"Peter visited me this morning, just before dawn," Hildoin said. "What he wants is to live here at Médard with his brother in Christ, Marcellinus, and their dear friend Tibertius. Einhard should be satisfied with the elbow of some obscure Burgundian bishop like St. Faro or the knee of Faro's sister Burgundofara. Bones that will bring dignity to his modest church without taxing its resources."

Hildoin crossed his legs. They were thin but well-toned.

"Einhard expects some sacred bones from you," Hildoin said. "So send him sacred bones. But not Peter and Marcellinus. They deserve better."

Hildoin recrossed his legs. He was a man of great presence and influence. Offending him would end my career. So I nodded and said, blasphemously, "Thy will be done," and consoled myself knowing that no matter whose bones I delivered, they would never be more than worthless substitutes. Let Hildoin claim whatever and whomever he wanted, so long as there was a drop of life in me, I'd fight to keep our saints and martyrs safe in Rome.

Hildoin beamed. "I'll send a good man with you," he said. "His name is Lehun. He's a priest, but he can think for himself. He'll bring Peter and Marcellinus to me at Saint Médard. He'll find a way."

"Better is the end than the beginning," I thought, with a nod to Ecclesiastes. But the end seemed very far away.

WHILE WE HAGGLED OVER TERMS—HILDOIN WANTED the bones before he parted with a single denier; I wanted half the fee up front—I agonized about my relationship with Einhard. He was as close to a friend as I had. He trusted me. He was a man of boundless pride but also of great faith and integrity, and I was about to betray him. Hildoin would announce to the world one day that Peter and Marcellinus had arrived safely at Saint Médard and were performing miracles by the hour. Einhard would assume correctly that I had sold him the priceless relics and then re-sold them to his archenemy Hildoin. The little man would despise me forever. He would call me a Judas. I would despise myself.

I asked God for guidance. "I'm a little child who doesn't know how to go out or come in," I told Him, quoting scripture.

The door slammed shut. I turned to look but no one was there.

A FEW DAYS LATER, THE THREE OF US—LEHUN, RATLEIG, and I—loaded our wagons and set off on the ancient road to Langres. As the great Abbey of Saint Médard dropped from view, a crow circled to our left, foretelling a successful journey.

Lehun hardly spoke. His eyes scanned the heavens wearily, as though he didn't know the blessed made their home there. His face was pale and narrow, with dry, thin lips. His eyes were dull as stones. He had lived a cloistered life in the shadow of Saint Médard, a stranger to the seasons, a novice to the art of living. Why, I wondered, had Hildoin chosen him for this arduous journey? Had he committed some unspeakable act for which he needed God's forgiveness through the intervention of the martyrs and saints? I could have pitied him, but I wasn't sure he wanted anything more than to be left alone.

LITTLE COULD HAVE CHANGED SINCE THE ROMANS pushed their way through this wilderness. There were a few cultivated clearings, some hillsides planted with vines, but otherwise only seamless forests bordered by wild heath, swamps, and bogs. At night we turned branches into tents and surrounded them with brambles to discourage the shaggy-haired bison and the wild black aurochs from attacking us with their huge horns. Lehun chewed garlic even while he slept. Ratleig was a devout Christian, but he was also a superstitious Frank who hung a buffalo tooth around his neck at night to ward off evil. On dark nights I wore one, too.

We all kept a lookout for wolf prints. A horse that stepped on one would be crippled for life. We used poisonous powders and baiting traps to catch a fox, but we were no match for the ferocious beast who was ravaging the countryside, punishing us for our sins. Only hours before we arrived in Langres, a rabid wolf stole into the church and bit off the leg of an adulterous girl as she knelt before the altar. The nave was splattered with her blood.

One night, under the influence of plum wine, Ratleig and I danced wildly around the fire. Lehun sat staring into the flames, poking the earth with a stick. Sparks scarred his face. He never budged.

ONCE WE CROSSED THE JURA MOUNTAINS WE MADE good time to Saint-Maurice. The wind blew as hard on Mont Joux as it did at Galilee. We arrived at Aosta safely, however, and followed the via Flaminia to Ivrea and Vercelli. Blessed by God, we rode without incident from Langres to Pavia in a month's time.

We ferried across the Po at Piacenza and continued across the Apennines to Tuscany. Ratleig came down with fever here. Every other day, in the late afternoon, his pulse increased, the blood drained from his face, and he began shaking with severe chills followed by sweating. This happened with such regularity, I had to believe he was in the grip of a devil who came by appointment to terrorize him. We broke alders over his head and poured absinthe down his throat to control his fever. His symptoms continued, so we tied bundles of herbs to his arms and legs and left him overnight in a hollow tree. Nothing worked. Finally, wide-eyed with terror, he confessed that he had enjoyed anal intercourse with his pregnant wife the third night of Lent, and pleaded with us to hurry toward the Eternal City so he could prostrate himself before the saints and beg forgiveness. By the next morning the evil spirit had fled, and he was his old self again. It was the sixth of the month. I chose to enter the gates on the seventh, seven being the number of the gifts of the Holy Ghost. Our trip from Soissons to Rome took just under three months.

TWENTY-ONE

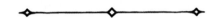

I'M MOST MYSELF WHEN I'M ALONE, FREE FROM SMILES AND THE TYRANNY OF CONVERSATION. BUT I AGREED TO LET LEHUN AND RATLEIG SHARE MY room with me. It was not an act of kindness. It was the only way I knew to keep an eye on them.

I left the men at home, told them to settle in, and rushed off to greet Peter and Marcellinus, stopping on the way to buy some fresh, snow-white calla lilies for their tomb. No homecoming could have been sweeter. The chapel was gloomy and choked with dust, but God had guarded my holy family during my long absence, and nothing was missing but a few votary lamps. My eyes pooled with tears. I was home again, among the blessed dead.

HOME IS NOT A WORD I WOULD EVER USE TO DESCRIBE the damp, drafty room I shared with my two unwelcome visitors.

They seldom spoke to me, or to each other. When I ordered them out the door each morning, just before sunrise, they went their separate ways. Lehun never bathed—I don't think it occurred to him that he needed to—and before long he had us all smelling like rancid cheese. His snoring could have wakened the dead. Ratleig washed, but only up to his neck. His oily hair stained my imported Turkish blankets.

Ratleig was determined to return home for the birth of his new child. But he refused to leave until he had visited every saint and martyr who had influence in heaven, and might please his cause before God. His mission dominated his life. At every church and chapel he left an offering—usually no more than a coin or two, but sometimes a chicken, a fig, a ball of wax. At the rate he was going, he'd soon have nothing left for anyone but prayers. Touched by the sincerity of his cause, I recommended him to a pilgrim guide, who listed all the important sites for him, and the most sensible order in which to visit them. This didn't bring him closer to God, but it saved him time and helped him fit more prayers into a day. I thought briefly of going into the guiding business as a sideline, but there was enough on my plate.

Lehun was never in a rush to go anywhere. He seemed content just hanging out at one of the lowlife bars near the Forum, throwing dice. I watched him from time to time. He had a set made from ivory that must have cost him a month's wages. Whether he played alone or with others didn't seem to matter to him. Winning or losing—it was all the same so long as he could gather up his die, shake them around in a small wooden box, and send them ricocheting around the table.

RATLEIG AND I WERE BOTH EAGER TO VISIT SAINT SILVIA, the patron saint of pregnant women, so one afternoon I brought him to her chapel, just outside the city walls. She had died of natural causes, but she was an influential saint who seems to have won God's favor, particularly on matters of childbirth. It pleased me that she came from a distinguished Roman family, and that her piety never stood in the way of her love of learning.

Ratleig knelt before a portrait of the saint and crossed himself. "Please, tell God about me," he implored her. "My name is Ratleig—let Him know I was here. I'm the one who left the flowers and figs. Remind Him He took away my first three children. If He's a just and loving God, ask Him to prove it and give me a healthy son."

The portrait had faded with time, but the saint's face remained ageless, animated, lit with a heavenly light. Her eyes turned toward me in a way that seemed to say, "Give thanks to your mother. She sacrificed her life so you could live. Give thanks, too, to Jesus, who gave His life so we could all live forever."

I tried to convince my visitors to substitute other martyrs for Peter and Marcellinus, but neither would hear of it, even with discounts and same-day delivery. "We only want what we came for," Ratleig said, gruffly. When I offered him the martyrs Diogenis, Bonifaccianus, and Festus, all below cost, he replied, in broken German, "Go fuck yourself." When I threw in assorted limbs of the blessed martyr Marius, his wife Martha, and their children Audifax and Habakkuk, he told me, under his breath, "Eat shit and die." He must have thought I couldn't understand broken Latin.

After a month I was ready to reclaim my room and, God willing, my life. Lehun didn't seem to care where he was, so long as he could roll his dice. Ratleig, running short on funds, was determined to be off soon. "I need to be home when my son opens his eyes," he told me. "I want to hear his first cry. Is there any sound more beautiful than the cry of a newborn child?"

It terrified me, the thought of waking Peter and Marcellinus before the Final Hour, forcing them to flee their ancient home and move into strange new quarters. But everyone knew their chapel along the via Labicana, and if I didn't move them soon, others would.

Act now, I told myself. And so that same night, under a new moon, I crept downstairs, determined to dig up the two martyrs and move them out of harm's way. I had just stepped into the street, however, when I was accosted by a messenger from Ingaold, the abbot of the famed Benedictine abbey of Farfa, only a few hours from Rome. He was under instructions to accompany me back to the abbey, where Ingaold hoped to buy twenty-four martyrs from me, including the Palestinian martyr Justin, the most revered Christian apologist of the second century—all but his severed head, which had rolled away and disappeared.

"The abbot has a fondness for women's ankles," the messenger told me. "But any sacred bones will do, so long as they're nicked or mutilated, and can perform their share of miracles. Speed is critical. A devil has infiltrated the monks' dormitory and asphyxiated several of them in their sleep."

A voice told me, "Return the messenger to Ingoald and promise to follow in a day or two. That will give you the time to transfer Peter and Marcellinus to other graves, deep in the catacombs, and to find some other, worthless bones for their chapel."

The devil had his own logic. "Don't disappoint Ingoald and risk losing a major new client," he told me, shortly before dawn. "Farfa is a big deal for a small-time salesman like you. A privileged relationship could keep you in furs for years. You could even afford an otter's cloak. And think of the time you'd save. Farfa is practically next door. Less travel means more time to perfect your recipes for sheep placenta, which you love, and soak your old bones in the public baths. You're not getting younger."

I felt jittery, leaving Peter and Marcellinus alone, unguarded, even for a few days. But the devil reassured me.

"They've been alone, unguarded, for more than five hundred years," he argued. "What's the likelihood He'll abandon them now?"

I wavered briefly and then, hoping for an easier, more indolent life, I threw away the keys to heaven and set off for Farfa. May God and His saints take pity on this sinner and return those keys to me some day.

WHEN I RETURNED HOME THREE DAYS LATER, I STEPPED into a hellish world of toppled chairs, broken plates, and shattered mugs. Everything reeked of piss and vomit. Rats feasted on putrid meat and stale chunks of bread and cheese. They glowered at me, and went on gnawing. Lehun and Ratleig were gone. Togas, sandals, blankets—all gone. Nothing remained but rows of worthless relics. I wanted to thank God for protecting them, but there was nothing worth protecting.

With a growing sense of foreboding, I grabbed a lantern and a couple of empty sacks and rushed through the dark, empty streets to the chapel of my beloved friends Peter and Marcellinus. A new moon hung like a scythe in the night sky. A cat crawled from a broken urn and stretched provocatively, like a whore. The air was as heavy as a dead man. I tore through the thick under-brush, crossed myself, and climbed down into the chapel of the blessed martyrs.

Black smoke curled up from an oil lamp and licked the graf-fiti on the wall. "Pray to the saints for victory," it said.

The altar stone stood on its side, leaning heavily against the tomb. I pushed my lantern into the darkness. Peter and Marcellinus were gone—all but a single large leg, glowing faintly in the dark. In their rush to be off, Ratleig and Lehun must have left it behind.

I raked my fingernails across my cheeks, drawing blood. No punishment was good enough for me. I had abandoned my holy family, and for what? A few lucrative orders? A bigger bedroom on a lower floor? Was my soul worth so little? My holy family was halfway to the Alps by now. I'd never see them again.

A spider crawled out from under the saint's leg. I lifted it reverently between my trembling fingers and released it into the dark. It was a holy spider now, having touched the living dead. "Woe to anyone who harms you," I said, as it scurried away.

The remaining bone, a gift apparently from God, was a shin or shank bone, the bone that supports most of our weight. I licked it. It had the smoky taste of pine chips after a fire.

I slid the leg into one of my sacks, half-expecting to be struck dead. Who, I wondered, had given me the right to intimacy with one of God's most beloved children? My hands were covered with holy dust. I licked them clean—fingers, hands, wrists. I ripped off my bloody nails with my teeth and swallowed the holy parings. Then I followed my flickering lantern to Tibertius's chapel nearby. Lehun and Ratleig had done their mischief here, too, but it didn't matter. Not to me. The bones they had stolen were as worthless as dust. The true remains were hidden where they couldn't be found—not by anyone but me or God.

As I headed home along the via Labicana, ancient chapels rose through the gloom like titans guarding the road to hell. "I'm beyond redemption," I told myself, echoing scripture. "Yet God can redeem me if He wishes. The wages of sin are death, yet Christ died so that sinners like me can live."

I listened for Christ's voice, but all I could hear was the howling wind.

Touching a shadow brings bad fortune, but as I walked home I deliberately stepped on one, taunting God to punish me. I could have saved Peter and Marcellinus any day since my return to Rome, and they would have remained together until the end of time, delighting in each other's presence, helping to keep our city strong and free.

Now they were gone. Until the end of time.

TWENTY-TWO

DOGS WERE TEARING AT THE GARBAGE IN MY COURTYARD AS I DRAGGED MYSELF UPSTAIRS. I HOPED MY SACRED LEG WOULD LIKE IT HERE, once I cleaned up the mess.

Moonlight lay across the room like a shroud. I placed my treasure on the table and lit a lamp. "This is not the way I live," I said out loud.

I worked quickly but methodically, sweeping the floor, discarding broken plates, returning bottles to their shelves. When I finished, I heard myself say, "That's better, don't you think?"

It was odd, talking to a leg—odd how natural it was, I mean, talking to it there in my room. It had numerous fractures. I couldn't say for certain whose it was, but the bones were small, and Peter was the younger of the two saints, so the leg must have been his. From that day, he was always Peter to me.

How strange it must feel, I thought, being separated from the body you were born with. I hoped that on the Final Day Peter would remind God that I had rescued him from his desecrated tomb and given him a loving home.

Thanks to me, Peter was no longer an orphan.

IT HAD BEEN A LONG, STRESSFUL DAY. I WAS BEYOND tired. I snuffed out the lamps, reached for Peter, and pulled him into bed with me. I kissed him goodnight and slipped him under the covers, amazed that I would be permitted to take such liberties with an intimate of God.

Peter gave off a low pulsating heat. He didn't resist me. He didn't say no. I drew him under my pillow and wrapped my arms around him. Fear became desire and turned to love. I fell asleep, delighting in his holy presence.

OUTSIDE MY WINDOW A DOVE BEGAN TO SING. *WA-WHO. Wa-who.* Peter and I clung tightly to its wings as it flew us to the gates of heaven. A young boy, his limbs intact, his body in the bloom of youth, waved warmly at us as we entered. It was my childhood friend and schoolmate, Luniso. I looked around in wonder. We were back in Republican Rome. The city rose in all its ancient glory, its buildings faced with marble and gold. Luniso and I wrestled and played hide-and-seek on the steps of the Palatine, as we had done when we were children.

The next thing I knew, it was morning and I was back in my room. I pulled the curtains back and peered at the family living behind the window across the street—eating, lusting, peering into my life as I was peering into theirs.

Sleep was out of the question. My cupboard was bare, so I returned Peter to the table, wrapped him in a blanket, and went shopping. Wanting to celebrate, and having a propensity for showing off, I returned with more than I could ever eat: A bag of white flour, eggs, pear cider, ground galangal, which I prefer to ginger, chickpeas, dark honey. I even bought a moorhen, which is divine when it's sprinkled with white pepper, but has hardly any meat and is impossible to skin. What was I thinking?

I used to scatter wildflowers on the tomb of the two martyrs, so I gathered a handful in an abandoned lot and brought them home with me. I had no idea how to arrange flowers, but I knew the colors I liked: blue, which is the color of truth and also of the sky, where God lives; and purple, the color favored by Roman emperors. I stayed away from red, the color of desire.

I couldn't wait to get upstairs. For the first time in my life, my room was not just a place to sleep or to escape the sun or rain. It was a home. It was *my* home. My heart beat expectantly as I bounded up the steps. Peter seemed anxious to hear how I had spent my time, down to the smallest detail, so I placed him on the table beside me. It was friendlier that way. This was not a tomb. I talked and talked, but sometimes I stopped talking and listened to the silence, which could be more intimate than talk.

IT WASN'T DIFFICULT IMAGINING WHAT HAD HAPPENED during my brief absence. Ratleig and Lehun must have paid dearly for the services of some half-baked priest, one of the Syrians or Greeks who prowled the catacombs, escorting pilgrims to the holiest tombs, luring them with the promise of heaven. The priest would have dug up the true relics of Peter and Marcellinus as well as the worthless bones I had substituted for Tibertius, and helped to pack them in the wagons for the long journey ahead. I thought for a moment of pursuing them, but they had almost a week's head start. My ancient horse Romulus would have collapsed from the strain.

· 819 AD ·

AS WEEKS PASSED, I BEGAN TO WONDER WHETHER MY beloved martyrs had safely crossed the Alps and were living in Hildoin's redoubtable abbey at Saint Médard or in Einhard's small, leaky church in Mulinheim. There was no way to know. Hildoin could have made off with all three martyrs, or only one, or part of one—a cheek, say, an elbow, or a chin. Einhard could have come away with nothing. I didn't really care. All that mattered to me was that Peter and Marcellinus were spending their days and nights together in the same chapel, reminiscing about their youth in Rome, consoling each other, chatting about their faith and the life to come. Their time in the grave would be less lonely if they had each other to say good morning and good night to.

I SPENT A FEW DAYS IN THE MARTYRS' DEFILED CHAPEL, cleaning up after my long absence. Peter and Marcellinus were gone, but not my obligation to care for the faithful who came to worship them. Sweeping cold, damp floors, filling lamps—the routine never changed. On Sundays I spread fresh lilies on the altar, compliments of a local flower merchant who thought I was a priest and agreed to provide them if I prayed for his soul at least once a week. I never deliberately forgot.

Fearing that Peter and Marcellinus would lose their following if their absence were known, I slipped into their empty tomb one night and buried the bones of two early Christians—a second-rate poet from the days of Honorius, and a fourth-century lawyer from Syracuse.

I worried now and then that Peter might miss his leg and want me to reunite it with the rest of his body in far off Mulinheim or Saint Médard—wherever he was. But Peter came to me regularly in my sleep and insisted in no uncertain terms that he felt safer and more loved alone with me than among the adoring crowds at Saint Médard, or in some neglected church in Gaul.

JUNE 2: THE DAY FINALLY ARRIVED, THE DAY I WAITED ALL year for—the day all days led to, when the faithful gathered to honor the martyrdoms of Peter and Marcellinus. It was a time of great celebration throughout Rome; but for me, who knew the martyrs were gone forever, it was also a time of loss and longing.

Spring was in the air, but nothing could erase the stench of the sick and dying as they pushed and clawed their way down into the chapel, hoping to claim a space near the martyrs. Pilgrims sprawled in back, guzzling wine and vomiting. Some of them, hoping for a miracle, swallowed water mixed with scrapings from the chapel walls. I kept an eye on everything.

I felt guilty, leaving Peter locked up alone in my room. He must have suffered terribly, being banned from the celebration of his own martyrdom. I hoped he understood that I couldn't watch over dozens of unruly visitors and look after him, too.

When I returned home it was close to dawn. I was exhausted but exhilarated. I had been where I had wanted to be, serving my holy family. I hoped Peter appreciated my efforts and would put in a good word for me with God.

TWENTY-THREE

THE SEASONS PASSED, AND I BECAME A NEW MAN—THAT IS TO SAY, I BECAME AN OLDER MAN WITH A NEW ROLE IN LIFE. I SELDOM TRAVELED more than a day or two from Rome. I avoided the Alps altogether. The mountain passes were for travelers who were younger, braver, and more fit than I was. I had a family to care for. Farfa was about the limit of my travels. Traders now came to me from distant cities. I lived less lavishly, but I needed less to live on. I lost business to Felix and other relic mongers, who milked the Frankish fairs for sales and new accounts. But I got by. I made a living most Romans would have envied. I could still afford all the pistachios I wanted, though I craved them less than before.

I made deals where I found them, a relic here, a relic there, always at fair market prices. If someone tried to bargain me down, I politely turned away. I was tired of life on the road, of hellos and goodbyes, of smiles I'd never see again. The world was still a place of wonder, full of possibilities, informed by God's light. But it had begun to lose some of its mystery and grandeur. I wanted to fall asleep each night on the same patch of earth, with the same pillow under my head, the same stars in the same familiar sky.

I had never had a family. I loved having one now. Peter made me feel I mattered. He sympathized with me when the day was too hot or too long, or when I was overcharged for prunes or bought a rotten pepper. He taught me that life is a veil of sorrow, and inspired me to raise my sights to the life to come. When I stubbed a toe, and cursed, he reminded me that there is no pain in heaven. He told me that no one would notice my homely face there, they would see only my soul, which was beautiful.

He was constantly telling me I could be better. "Keep your clothes washed," he said, and "Don't slouch so much." He reminded me that men lose their hair as they age, that genitals come in different sizes, and that drinking is no substitute for life. When I misbehaved, he scolded me. When I behaved, he promised to let God know what a solid, warmhearted fellow I was, and to ask Him to forgive my trespasses at the final hour. He taught me not to worry so much about small things—spilling a few drops of table wine on my beige tunic, say, or misplacing a towel—for life is a shadow, a passing moment, and whatever is real and lasting has yet to come.

As a relic sanctifies a church, so Peter sanctified my home, transforming it into a House of God.

ONE STARLESS NIGHT, AS I WAS WALKING HOME ALONE, swinging my lamp along the via Labicana, I was assaulted by the smell of sulfur and the sight of Emperor Charles standing in the buff in his steaming bath, teaching his pale, young students the dialogues of Alcuin.

"Now, to what is man like?" the emperor said.

"To an apple on a tree."

"And how is he placed?"

"Like a lantern in the wind."

Alcuin had it right. We live for a moment and are gone. The apple falls. The wind blows out the light. But the martyrs give us hope of eternal life. They hear our pleas and carry them to heaven. They represent us at God's throne. The miracles they perform remind us that there is a living God and a life to come. There must be, or our days would have no purpose, and that would be unthinkable.

I looked around. Charles was gone. So were the stars. Church bells rang, summoning me home, as they had long ago, when I was a child, alone on the Palatine.

Lehun and Ratleig had been gone almost six months when news reached me that all three martyrs—Peter, Marcellinus, and Tibertius—were with Hildoin at Saint Médard, healing the sick and lame. Einhard still claimed that Peter and Marcellinus were with him in Mulinheim, but only a few pilgrims had ever heard of Einhard, and they avoided him and his leaky church as they made their way to Rome. It was another humiliating loss for Einhard, another win for Hildoin.

The situation was an embarrassment to Rome, of course. It was not unusual for two churches to claim relics of the same saint—a finger here, a foot there—but it was scandalous for two neighboring churches to claim identical remains. Faith went only so far.

IT SEEMED A LIFETIME HAD PASSED SINCE I HAD FIRST seen Godel crouching in her garden among her fava beans and vetches. Had she ever existed? At times she seemed no more than a pleasant dream, an earthy smell, a feeling with shape and color. The Alps rose silently between us, a great insurmountable wall of ice. Had her husband returned to torment her? Was she still alive? Was her son? I remembered the joy on his sweet young face when I blew music through a blade of grass, but the memory was dim.

AS THE DAYS SHORTENED, AND SUMMER SUCCUMBED TO fall, my relationship with Peter began to change. My shyness left me, and so did my sense of awe. Slowly, imperceptibly, he wove himself into the fabric of my life, and I began to take his presence for granted, like sunlight or the air we breathe. At times, while I was kneading bread or pouring wine, I forgot that he was in my room, lying on the table or under the bed, so close we could almost touch. I would go off to shop or wander along the river, leaving him exposed on the table. It was careless of me. While I listened to Virgil in the Forum or strolled through the ruins on the Palatine, reminiscing about more innocent times, any stranger could have broken in and stolen him.

When Peter first arrived, I tried to create an atmosphere that was worthy of him. Now I often fell asleep surrounded by dirty plates and dishes. "Yes, I know," I'd say, "I'll wash up in the morning."

I continued to bring him flowers, but sometimes I forgot to water them, and left them wilting on the table. I still prayed to him every night, but not on my knees. The floor was hard. I slept late when I should have been in his chapel at dawn, serving beer to early risers.

I worshipped Peter, I was a lost soul without him. But it grated on me that everything I did was under his gaze and subject to his approval. It was hard work, always trying to be better than I was. I didn't always want to be my best self. I would have given my life for Peter, but at times my tiny room felt crowded. I wanted to fall asleep with him in my arms, the way a prisoner longs to embrace his jailer, the holder of the keys. But his love was also at times a burden, requiring more of me than I had to give, or wanted to give.

I missed my days and nights on the road, when I could exhaust myself and go to bed tired, staying in one place when I was content, moving on when I was not. I missed the hellos and goodbyes, though they added up to nothing, and the blue skies with their window into heaven. Life had no meaning without my holy friend and lover Peter, but there were times when I needed to escape his gaze. Feeling restless and pinned down, I sometimes went outside and walked the streets—wherever my legs took me. I walked home slowly, trying to put off the inevitable return; but as I climbed my stairs, my heart quivered with excitement. "I'm here," I'd sing out, half expecting a reply.

TWENTY-FOUR

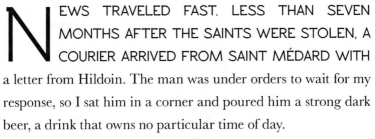

NEWS TRAVELED FAST. LESS THAN SEVEN MONTHS AFTER THE SAINTS WERE STOLEN, A COURIER ARRIVED FROM SAINT MÉDARD WITH a letter from Hildoin. The man was under orders to wait for my response, so I sat him in a corner and poured him a strong dark beer, a drink that owns no particular time of day.

Let Hildoin speak for himself. He always does.

To the Holy Roman deacon Deusdona
Hildoin, greetings

The faithful believe that Tibertius is now on display in Saint Peter's, performing miracles by the hour, and that Peter and Marcellinus are gracing Einhard's church at Mulinheim. This is perversity. All three martyrs are here with me at Saint Médard, giving eyes to the blind, and wealth and fame to my

abbey. What games are you and Einhard playing with the truth?
Deceit doesn't wear well on men of the cloth.

I know the story. My man Lehun filled me in. He was
there. Frustrated by your endless delays, he and Ratleig took
matters into their own hands and hired a young priest to
help them dig up the three martyrs one moonless night. Dawn
was still several hours away when Lehun and Ratleig tiptoed
upstairs, clutching the priceless treasure. Tempers flared as they
began to pack, each claiming Peter and Marcellinus for himself.
The mood grew tense and ugly. Sharing the bones was not an
option either man would entertain. They would have come to
blows if Lehun hadn't stepped in and proposed an ingenious
solution—a simple game of dice, with the two martyrs going to
the winner.

Ratleig's response was no surprise. "God abhors games of
chance," he proclaimed.

Lehun had heard this argument a thousand times before,
and could respond in his sleep. "Nothing happens by chance," he
said. "How could it, if there's a God? We may throw the dice,
but God determines how they fall. Proverbs 16:33."

It took Lehun only a moment to draw the die from a small
box and send them flying across the table. The fine points of the
game elude me, but there was no debate—Ratleig had lost. Lehun
whistled as he wrapped the bones in sheets, carried them down-
stairs, and locked them in chests at the bottom of his wagon.

"My life is over," Ratleig mumbled.

It was an optimistic assessment, if you ask me.

This is a long letter, even for a church father. Let me be brief. Dawn came, and Lehun set off for Saint Médard with the remains of the three martyrs—Peter, Marcellinus, and Tibertius. Ratleig rumbled along behind. He had lost two of Rome's most venerable martyrs to a set of dice, but his faith in God remained unshaken. "I would have won if we could have kept playing," he told Lehun as they huddled around the fire one night. "The world isn't ruled by chance. Eventually I would have won."

What Ratleig didn't know was that Lehun played with loaded dice and lost only when he wanted to prove he wasn't invincible. I let him get away with it from time to time. It discouraged gambling in the abbey. The two of us often played late at night, waiting for Mass. The die we used were mine.

Ratleig showed his true character when he plucked the bones of two ancient travelers from a raging stream one night and, on his return to Mulinheim, presented them to Einhard as the remains of Peter and Marcellinus. When Einhard saw them, he leaned forward and kissed them on the mouth and cheeks. Then he burst into tears of joy.

Such is the power of faith.

The worthless bones are enshrined today in a chapel in Mulinheim Abbey. Pilgrims seek them out, hoping for long life, long legs, a bumper crop of leeks—whatever it is that pilgrims seek. It pains me that so many men and women of good faith are being hoodwinked by Einhard, when the true martyrs are here

*with me at Saint Médard, performing miracles faster than you
can say "Deus magnus est."*

*It will take a giant leap of faith for me to ever trust you
again, knowing that without Lehun's intervention the martyrs would still be in Rome, awaiting their deliverance. Your
devilish delays support my fear that, after all is said and done,
you are nothing but a glorified relic monger, preying on the
faithful. Your reputation for deceit follows you. Or should I say,
"precedes you"?*

*But all is not lost. If God can forgive sinners, I can too.
Please know, therefore, that should you ever want to reclaim
my trust, or, dare I say it, my affection, there are countless
other saints and martyrs you could procure for me, all of
whom would move to Saint Médard in the twinkling of an eye.
Saints who specialize in specific ailments, the so-called patron
saints, are of particular interest to me. We are living in an age
of specialization, and the saint who can cure general ills is
in less demand than he was in more unsophisticated times. I
could, for example, use a limb or two of Mary's mother, whose
prayers on behalf of infertile women are said to have special
influence in heaven. I also have a spare chapel for a relic of
Saint Agatha, the patron saint of breast ailments, which strike
so many of our women in Soissons, especially the rich. I would
ask God to look kindly on you if you could locate a relic of
Saint James, who is known to cure arthritis. I would get down
on my knees and pray to him myself if I weren't so stiff.*

My courier will be in Rome for a few weeks, recovering

from his arduous journey. He has the right to negotiate for me, so once you agree on terms, he'll arrange to send the holy relics to Saint Médard. Lehun is out of the picture. We've parted ways. He no longer serves me—or God. I asked him to join you because he was a lost soul and I hoped that in the Eternal City, under the influence of so many powerful martyrs and saints, he would find his way back to God. How you subverted him and poisoned his mind I'll never know, but a few weeks after his return to Saint Médard, he converted to Judaism, took the Jewish name Eleazor, had himself circumcised, married a Jewish seamstress from Soissons, and set off to Spain. Spain! I was speechless.

I told the messenger that if he returned in two weeks, I'd have a bill and a list of deliverables for him. He turned and left without a thank you for the beer. Alone again, I immersed myself in Hildoin's note, trying to separate truth from conjecture. Lehun would have told Hildoin anything to satisfy his own dark ambitions. Hildoin knew only what Lehun told him, but he never doubted for a moment that the martyrs wanted to move in with him at Saint Médard and would be miserable anywhere else.

So we create a world in our own corrupt image.

I was disappointed not to learn what became of Ratleig when he returned to Mulinheim. Did he hand over the remains of the three martyrs to Einhard, as he was charged to do? Did he deliver substitutes? Whether he gambled the martyrs away or delivered them to Einhard, I didn't really know or care. All that mattered to me was that his wife gave birth to a healthy boy who would some day bear children of his own.

The sky was overcast. I lifted my arms in prayer.

DAYS RUSHED BY AS I RAN ABOUT ROME, TRYING TO quench Hildoin's thirst for relics. I wanted to please him. He was an important man. Saint Agatha was in Catania, however, and I wasn't about to go relic-hunting in Sicily. I was too far along in life for that. I did, however, buy Hildoin the platter Saint Agatha used to carry her ample breasts after they had been hacked off by her lowborn Roman suitor Quintianus. She must have sold the platter or given it away after her breasts were reattached by St. Peter. I found the platter in a secondhand furniture store on a back lane in Trastevere. I wouldn't have known what it was if the owner hadn't told me.

I couldn't find even the smallest sliver of Saint Anne. The Eastern Church is more devoted to her than we are, and her remains are safely guarded in Constantinople. I could have provided Saint Anne's left foot, but I had purchased it from a priest of dubious repute, and it was misshapen, like a club foot, and I would never have insulted the Virgin's mother, or the Holy Church, for a quick sale.

I wasn't sure whether Hildoin wanted James the Greater or James the Lesser. People always confuse the two, which can get a deacon into hot water. The Greater was the son of Salome and the fisherman Zeberdee. The other was the Apostle. James the Great wasn't greater, he was just taller. Most Frankish clerics want to own a part of him because his remains are in Spain and hard to locate. A heavenly voice led me to a church not far from Saint Peter's, where I obtained a few hairs from James's ample beard and a splinter from his long, thin staff. The hairs were credible because they were orange-red, the colors of his mercurial temperament. The splinter came from a cedar tree found only in the wooded valleys of central Andalusia.

I pulled together an inventory of seventeen saints and martyrs I planned to deliver, estimating fees and adding a modest surcharge for increases in overhead. I threw in the following note, responding to Hildoin's groundless accusations against my integrity. My words balanced modesty with pride.

To the Holy Archchaplain Hildoin
Deusdona, greetings

I'm sending you a list of saints and martyrs I'm prepared to provide, once we agree on terms. As you can imagine, they're all delighted to relocate. "Saint Médard!" I overheard one of them say. "We're going to Saint Médard!"

Few of the saints you seek are buried near Rome, so I drew on my private collection, authenticating relics with whatever official seals and letters I could find. You're at liberty to cross off whatever bones are not documented to your satisfaction, without charge or question, so long as they remain in the same pillow you received them in, and none of the bones has been further damaged or shows additional wear.

In your letter, which gives new meaning to the word exhaustive, you asked me to explain how Peter and Marcellinus could be on display at Mulinheim when their remains are in Saint Médard. I would satisfy you if I could, but as you know, Ratleig and Lehun ran off with the martyrs while I was out of town, serving God. When I returned, the thieves had gone. All that remained were broken dishes and empty wine flasks, left behind without so much as a thank you or I'm sorry. Which relics ended up in whose hands? Who delivered what to whom? These are questions others will have to answer. I wasn't there.

You accuse me of failing to turn over the relics in a timely manner, of stalling on the goods, as my Jewish friends would say. But how could I, in all good conscience, have delivered them to a crook like Lehun? He was a man without God who devoted his days to booze and gambling. Peter and Marcellinus would never have put themselves in Lehun's hands, and I would never have entrusted them to his. This was no cakewalk. They were crossing the Alps.

You asked about Tibertius. A few of his sacred limbs may remain here in Rome, performing miracles at Saint Peter's. I don't pretend to know. But all men of God should be thankful for the saints who remain among us, for it is through them that God spreads His net wide, hoping to catch as many sinners as he can. These are perilous times. Without our saints and martyrs, the Eternal City will fall. Christ's army needs all the soldiers it can muster, alive or dead.

You have most of Tibertius. Two-thirds, I would say. More than half. Maybe three-fourths. Be grateful. The saint will be whole again one day, strolling with us through the fields of heaven. For now, Tibertius adds luster to your life and your abbey. Saint Médard thrives.

May we meet again on the last day, if not sooner.

By the bye, if Lehun hasn't departed for Spain, I'd consider it a favor to purchase his foreskin. I assume he no longer needs it. It would be a curiosity indeed. Perhaps the Jew who circumcised him knows where it is.

Hildoin's notary returned before I knew it, and I sent him off with my reply. I also left him a gift I had received from a supplier in the Holy Land: a small pine box packed with clods of earth that had been sanctified by Our Savior's feet as he trudged toward Calvary. The box contained a sheet of parchment stamped with a cross—a nice touch. One of Hildoin's assistants spent the better part of a day spooning the holy soil into tiny packets and selling them to the faithful. The packets went fast, even when Hildoin tripled the price.

A FEW DAYS LATER I WAS VISITED BY A MESSENGER FROM Mulinheim. His right arm shook wildly, as though it were possessed by a devil, so I made him stand out in the rain and pass his letter across the threshold. It was from Einhard, requesting additional relics. I told the man to return in two months, and I encouraged him to spend every free moment visiting Rome's most venerated churches and begging the saints and martyrs for forgiveness. I had no clue what sins he had committed, but judging by his powerful tremors, he had much to atone for. I opened Einhard's note as soon as I was alone.

To the holy Roman deacon Deusdona
Einhard, greetings

Let me get to the point. My spleen is on fire, and I have no patience for words or for the life of the mind.

I greeted the arrival of Peter and Marcellinus with the greatest joy and expectation, but I've been utterly disappointed in the hopes that I placed in their intercession. Hildoin claims the martyrs are his, not mine, and that they have taken up residence at Saint Médard at their own request. Pilgrims, he says, are flocking there in record numbers, and filling the offering plates in record speed. Meanwhile, contributions to my new lead roof continue to dry up. Those who swore to share the burden ignore their obligation.

I'm writing as a man of God and a lover of the truth to tell you what took place in your home the night before Ratleig and Lehun began their journey home. I know. Ratleig told me. He was there.

Ratleig had packed up the martyrs and was ready to carry them downstairs to his wagon, when Lehun, aware that time was running out, offered to buy the bones for a hundred pieces of silver. The money could only have come from Lehun's boss Hildoin, for only a man of the cloth could have been so unprincipled and well-endowed. Ratleig, as honest and God-fearing a man as ever walked the earth, turned away, cursing. Lehun then tried to win the martyrs in a game of chance. Morra, it's called— one-two-three-shoot. A game for children. Can you imagine? Ratleig would have none of it. He slipped the three martyrs into separate muslin pillows and buried them under piles of clothes in the back of his wagon. He would not let Lehun help.

The two men traveled together for three months, bound by hatred and a will to survive the fearsome mountain passes. Before they parted—Ratleig to Mulinheim, Lehun to Médard— Lehun plucked the bones of two travelers from a frozen swamp, intending, once he was home, to present them to Hildoin as the remains of Peter and Marcellinus. These worthless bones are now on display in the ornate Chapel of Peter and Marcellinus in Saint Médard, and Archchaplain Hildoin gloats—gloats!—over his latest acquisition.

I can't compete with Hildoin, but it would serve God, and restore my faith in you, if you would provide my modest church with a few additional limbs—a foot, a thigh, a toe—anything that would draw an occasional pilgrim back to my beloved village. I'd also welcome any saint or martyr who can reduce my kidney pain, which is excruciating and blocks out all reasonable thought. Among those who come to mind are Saint Benedict of Nursia, who was born to Roman nobility, and Saint Ursus, who founded the monastery of Monte Cassino. If they were here with me, I'd pamper them to distraction.

Benedict and Ursus both died of natural causes, but they're said to be among God's favorites. If on your travels you chance upon them, or any part of them, send them my way. I'll pay dearly. Good health knows no price.

As for Ratleig's baby, he died in childbirth, before he could be baptized. I thought you'd want to know. The mother lives, though in a sorry state. It's sad to think the boy will never go to heaven or meet God face to face. Perhaps Ratleig will try again. It seems he hasn't given up hope, for he still goes to Mass each morning and evening, and faithfully recites his prayers. He keeps telling me he killed his son, but I take this as the ravings of an honest Christian overcome with grief. He asked me once to excommunicate him, but how could I damn someone whose only sin was trying to bring life into the world? A few days ago he asked my permission to throw himself in a briar patch. I refused him, as the sight of his blood streaming down his body would have brought him nothing but the most exquisite pleasure. He refused to leave me without some sort of punishment, so I told him to repeat twenty psalms on his knees each day for twenty days, with his arms extended in a cross. I also made him abstain from juicy meats for the rest of his life. I regret this punishment, as juicy meat before copulation leads more often to the birth of a boy, and he is likely to try to have one again soon.

The sun dipped behind a dark cloud and for a moment the world seemed an unfamiliar place. Ratleig's son was dead. He would never see God, never stroll in Christ's garden and hear

Our Lord play His seven-string lyre. The gates of heaven were closed to him forever. I thought of the many shapes sadness can take over a lifetime, and I prayed to God that I would never have a child of my own.

I made my way downstairs and went where I always did when I needed to think and be alone—to the broken streets of ancient Rome. Most of the area was deserted and in ruins, the province of paupers and wild beasts, but it was where I had always gone as a child to escape my teachers and to learn what it meant to be me.

GOD LED ME TO THE BASILICA OF SANTA MARIA Maggiore, high above the city, on the summit of Esquiline Hill. When I reached the altar, I fell to my knees. I had brought Ratleig here several months before, and we had prayed together to the Virgin Mother to bring him a healthy child. Why had she ignored him? Was his offering too paltry? Did Lehun, the Devil's henchman, speak the truth when he claimed that the sounds of clinking coins mean more to our saints and martyrs than prayers? How could it be? Christ loved the poor. "The poor are the heirs of the Kingdom," he said. "The Lord hears the poor."

I wondered whether God, being omniscient, had looked forward in time and judged Ratleig's baby by the sins he would have committed, had he lived. Perhaps Ratleig sold the martyrs to Lehun or lost them to him in a game of chance, as Hildoin claimed, and the baby was punished for his father's transgressions. Or perhaps the baby died for his father's father's disobedience, or his father's father's father's, and so on back through all the generations. We all bear the burden of Adam's sin.

I headed home wondering for the hundredth time why God had taken Ratleig's baby but allowed me to live. Did He expect me to lead a life that justified my mother's death? Had I disappointed Him? Were the gates of heaven closed to me too?

I had sinned. I knew. I had spilled my seed in a holy crypt, and not repented. I had touched a woman's breasts while she slept. For more than a year I worked for slave-traders, trafficking in human flesh. For a few coins, I had abandoned my most beloved friends Peter and Marcellinus, robbing Rome of two of her most powerful protectors.

I had done some terrible things. Only a liar or a fool could deny it. But I was also God's servant. I had spent the larger part of my life spreading His gospel. The bones I sold were worthless as dust, but they brought the hope of redemption to an ignorant and superstitious people, and reinforced the moral authority of Rome. The Franks believed in these powers and were inspired by them, and who is to say they were wrong or misled?

I sold every name in the canon, but it was only the names I sold, never the saints and martyrs themselves. If I ever disturbed them in their sleep, it was only to shelter them within the city walls, under the wing of the Church, or to hide them in unmarked graves so robbers could never find them. I never wavered in my mission to keep our saints and martyrs here in Rome, where they could protect us from floods and disease, and give us the courage and strength to defeat the enemy. Let Hildoin dismiss me as a relic monger—thanks to me, the Franks could now see a world beyond their own. I never owned a sword, but I did the work of a thousand swords, capturing men's hearts and souls. Winning them to God.

It's said that the relic below the altar of San Prassada is a fragment of Lazarus' nose. In truth, it's the back of a moorhen's skull. I gave it to the abbot as a thank-you for an inspired Christmas dinner several winters ago. I was praying in the same sanctuary recently when a man possessed by an evil spirit crawled over to the relic like a crab, and touched it. As the spirit fled, the man let out a blood-curdling scream, rose slowly, and disappeared into the street.

"God works in many wonderful ways," I told myself. "Praise Him."

WOLVES HOWLED IN THE DARKNESS. I PICKED UP MY pace. This was not the Imperial City I had learned about in school. A pack of howling dogs loped into a deserted building. Homeless men and women prowled the streets, picking through garbage. Others huddled around makeshift campfires, trying to stay warm. A beggar extended his bowl to me. I crossed the street. I had several pieces of silver, but no small change.

As I made my way home, my mind was deluged with images of Ratleig's wife cradling her dead child in her arms. I also saw myself, a newborn child, lying in my mother's blood, shedding tears she'd never see.

Craving the solace of family and friends, I rushed home to

Peter. Without pausing to wash, I slid his chest out from under my bed, withdrew the sacred leg, and placed it on the table beside me. Through the window came the sounds of breaking plates. My neighbor Sergius and his wife were at it again. She screamed and cursed him. Eventually they quieted down. I could hear their soft laughter, and then, later, their heavy breathing. They sounded like bison in heat. Poets call it love. I lowered my head beside Peter's leg and drifted off to sleep. Whether it was the sleep of the blessed or the damned, I can't say.

FOR TWO WEEKS I RUSHED FRANTICALLY AROUND THE city, gathering relics for Einhard, trying to impress him with my intelligence and speed. I began with the most accessible ones— Benedict of Nursia, Ursus, Calistus, Alexandrus, Maximus, and the virgin Basilla.

A local priest claimed to possess Benedict's right hand. The man had an open, honest face, so I decided not to question his integrity. A thumb was missing, but it was a noble hand, long and refined, exactly what you would expect from someone born of ancient Roman stock. With the help of a local seamstress, I located the lower jaw of Saint Ursus. His back teeth were worn almost to the bone, like the teeth of my horse Romulus, but he would do.

The third-century martyr Callistus was a personal favorite. Before he became pope he served as a deacon, in charge of the cemetery on the Appian Way. Some say he was easy on sinners. I prefer to believe he was forgiving. His chapel was close by, in

Travestere, so I walked over and bought two of the martyr's ribs from the caretaker, an indigent priest who had to be summoned from home. Both bones were intact. One was whiter and more frail than the other, which was odd, but in my line of work it's not smart to ask too many questions.

Maximus, of course, was not the Confessor from Constantinople—that was another Maximus. This one was Saint Cecilia, who lived near the church in Trastevere. I found the little that remained of her—a fractured scapula—in a forgotten chapel in the same cemetery as Saint Callistus. She was never martyred, but she was of patrician rank and her brother, I learned, was none other than my friend Tibertius. Cecilia had been betrothed to a young pagan, but she changed her mind on her wedding day, and consecrated her virginity to God. The priest I spoke to wouldn't part with any of her, so I bought her bridal veil. It looked almost new, which was odd for a five-hundred-year-old strip of silk. But the cloth was embroidered with the image of an organ, which gave it credibility. Cecilia is the patron saint of musicians.

ALL ANYONE COULD TELL ME ABOUT ALEXANDRUS WAS his name, which is listed in the Canon of the Mass. I wasn't about to complain. If no one knew him, no one could question me. I wrapped one of his limbs, a fractured shinbone, in an expensive muslin pillow, and hired an experienced tailor to embroider it with an Old Gaelic "A." I paid him with a vial of lamp oil from Saint Gaudentius in Brescia. All my best oil came from nuts and grains grown in Saint Gaudentius. It was strictly wholesale, and delivery was thrown in when I bought in bulk.

I was delighted to spread the fame of the martyr Basilla, an orphan of imperial lineage. She had been pledged to Pompey himself, but, like Cecilia, she had converted at the final hour, and been rewarded with the blade of the emperor's sword. I crept down inside Basilla's chapel one dark night and snapped off one of her ribs. The sword marks were unmistakable, tripling the weapon's value.

When Einhard's messenger returned, his arm was still shaking wildly, so I settled up with him quickly in the hallway, at the bottom of the stairs, and sent him packing. God's world is perfect. Einhard's messenger was not. I tried to put as much space between us as I could. I felt guilty, not offering him anything to drink, but not badly enough to call him back.

I lay alone in my room that night, trapped in my body, unable to sleep. A solitary star flickered in the sky, reminding me of Charles's palace in Aachen, shining in the dark. Everything moves, everything changes, I told myself. But God does not move or change. Neither do His laws. Only man has changed from the perfection of God's creation, and man must change again before that perfection will again be his.

Spoken like a priest, I mused. Perhaps I've missed my calling.

From time to time I thought I saw Godel stooped over in a field of vetches and imagined myself making a life with her, raising cows and children. But the die was cast, as Lehun wouls have said. I loved God's world, but I loved God more.

Filling occasional orders from Einhard and Hildoin hardly covered my expenses, but other requests kept coming in from every corner of the kingdom. A monk from Fulda named Theolmar waited with childlike impatience in a Frankish hostel near Saint Peter's while I satisfied his need for Alexander, Fabian, and the back of Urban's skull. I had already sold five of these skulls; this would have to be the last.

I continued to sell the occasional saint or martyr, but as the relic trade grew, the opportunities for fraud expanded and so did the pressure on me to authenticate the bones I sold. When my margin was low, it was hardly worth the effort.

More competition also meant less bargaining power. My prices were always fair, but if a buyer didn't like them, he knew he could go elsewhere. When I complained to Hildoin about his low—some would say insulting—offer for the knee of Sainte Foy, he told me what I could do about it.

Since unauthenticated bones were increasingly hard to sell, I supplemented my income with pilgrim badges and wine mugs stamped with the Holy Cross. Profits on medallions and other religious keepsakes were small but steady, and added up over time. Every pilgrim was grateful for something tangible that he could carry home and remember his visit by, and pray to in times of famine and disease.

TWENTY-FIVE

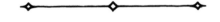

L IFE WENT ON, AND MY BONES, LIKE MY CART, BEGAN TO CREAK. IN THE PAST, EVERY DAY HAD HAD ITS OWN STORY, ITS OWN BEGINNING AND end. Now the days flowed together—all but Sunday, when I brought Peter out from under the bed, and we broke bread together around the kitchen table.

Over time, Hildoin and Einhard became major customers again. At the end of the day they must have decided that I was not the most reliable dealer, but I was more reliable than anyone else.

I sent Einhard a good part of holy Felicity, mother of seven sons, and an arm of the holy virgin and martyr Emmerentiana. Emmerentiana is usually portrayed clutching a bouquet of lilies, so I pressed a few between her fingers. To prolong their lives, I picked the flowers in the morning, just after the dew evaporated from the leaves, and hung them up in a warm dark place to dry.

I liked pleasing Einhard, but I would have made the same effort for anyone who trusted me and believed in God. I also satisfied Einhard's request for the remains of Saint Hermes, a freed slave whose name is invoked against mental illness. Why Einhard wanted Hermes I was loathe to ask.

I never gave up on the idea of delivering relics to Einhard in person, and dropping in on Hildoin on my way home. But to what end? They would be the same two men they had always been, only grayer, shorter, and more gnarled. Each had his own grasp on truth, and neither would ever let go until the final hour.

ON A BONE-CHILLING MORNING, WHEN THE DAMPNESS cut through me like a knife, a woman down the street gave birth to a child with webbed feet. Within an hour, our detested Father Paschal was gone. I joined the furious crowds blocking the streets so he couldn't be interred near Peter. He was left unburied until our next Father, Eugenius, took pity on him and found him a small corner grave in the crypt of Saint Pressede.

Eugenius had a tiny mouth and large, dazed, Byzantine eyes. He stroked his thick, wiry beard even during Mass. He had more hair than Paschal, evidence of a less religious temperament. His father was Boemund, a Lombard.

You can imagine the horror all true Romans felt when Eugenius, hoping to pay off his political debts, began selling our saints and martyrs in terrifying numbers, largely to Frankish noblemen, who had come to Christ late in life and thought they could buy redemption with a coin and a prayer.

As God turned away in anger, our world fell apart. The Saracens devastated all the land around Barcelona. Crete fell to the Andalusians. The Bulgars ravaged the borders of Upper Pannonia. I saw battle lines and shifting lights in the sky.

ONE SWELTERING SUMMER DAY, GOD TOOK EUGENIUS from us. No one mourned. I eagerly awaited his successor, Valentine, who was born in Rome's aristocratic fifth district and was known for his eloquence and looks. His privileged status couldn't stay death's hand, however, and thirty-six days later he was gone. What I remembered most about him were his gentle features and his unruly white hair standing up on either side of his tonsured head, like angel wings. He was our hundredth pope, more or less, so I bought a coin struck in his name as a keepsake.

Valentine's successor, our current Pope Gregory, also came of strong Roman stock. It was not God's plan to hide his saints and martyrs in unmarked graves, so I returned Tibertius to Gregory. "God will reward you with good health and an extra year or two in the Book of Life, " the pope promised me on my first visit.

"Let's make it two," I joked.

Romans poured joyfully into the streets when they heard that their beloved Tibertius was not imprisoned at Saint Médard, as rumor had it, but was still in Rome, performing miracles. He was given his own venerable chapel near Saint Peter, where the faithful came and prayed for protection from the Saracens, who were advancing toward our gates with impunity. Tibertius gave us all great hope and courage in a time of need.

It was, at best, an uncertain time. While Louis's children waved their jewel-studded swords at each other, the Saracens marched toward Rome. An attack was imminent. All our hopes rested with Gregory, who was teaching us how to fend for ourselves. Under his direction, our harbor at Ostia was reinforced, its walls heightened and surmounted with catapults. It was strange, wonderful work for a man of God.

Gregory was also organizing a powerful army under the duke of Tuscany. The soldiers were gathering in Beneventum. I decided to go there too, and join the fight against the infidel. Like King Charles—like Charles the Great—I'd be a friend to friends, and an enemy to enemies. Lyres and doves would have to wait. The world was now. The Saracens were at our gates.

I rushed downstairs and out into the biting rain. It was not far to the great central market—the one that had drawn me as a child to its exotic smells and colors. I was not looking for spices and silks now, but for a second-rate sword. The one I settled on was old and dull. It couldn't slice a pig's ass. But it was an honest piece of work. It wasn't made for a king, but I wasn't a king. The cross-guard was short but the grip was inlaid with small metal plates and wound with thread. The pommel was carved in the shape of a fierce, two-headed dragon. Great men give swords to their sons when they reach manhood. Perhaps my father would have given me one like this.

I smiled wistfully and returned the sword to its owner. The last time I had used a weapon I was an eight-year-old schoolboy playing with a wooden stick on the Palatine. "It's me, Augustus," I had shouted, but no one had answered, no one had heard.

THERE ARE MANY WAYS OF FACING AN ENEMY, I REMINDED myself, and I set out to prove it at Beneventum. I'd station myself among our men, a safe distance from the front lines, and as they prepared for battle, I'd sell them medallions of Christ the Warrior, brandishing a cross. They'd rush to buy these symbols of their faith, and hang them around their necks as they marched into battle. Soldiers in Christ's army, they would advance fearlessly against the enemy and risk death—embrace death if necessary— to win God's approbation.

A soldier will give his last coin to cheat death and greet his family and friends again after the battle. There was no doubt I could make a fortune selling medallions. But I refused to take advantage of someone else's hopes and fears, and pledged at least half my profits to burying the dead.

ARMED WITH FAITH AND A NEW SENSE OF MISSION, I walked briskly to the home of a Greek merchant I had known since childhood, and bought several hundred medallions, packing and delivery included in the fee. Then I went off in search of last-minute supplies—wild peas, fava beans, eggs, wheat, wine, smoked cod. Always too much.

It was early evening when I dragged myself upstairs to my

room, perhaps for the last time. I could hear Saint Sergius barking at his wife in the room below. My relics could stay where they were—they had no real value. Romulus and I would be off at dawn.

For a moment I considered returning Peter to his ancient chapel on the via Labicana, but I decided against it. Who would choose to wait out the final hour lying among strangers? I thought of burying him in Tibertius's tomb, but I might never return, and both men would be ignored and eventually forgotten.

"It's best for us to stick together," I told Peter, with a friendly grimace. "I'll watch over you, you'll watch over me. It's a win-win situation."

I couldn't sleep that night. I kept feeling the point of a sword ripping through my flesh. Blood rushed from the wound, the color of roses. The day was just rising out of the darkness when I returned to my table, dipped my quill in ink, and began to scribble a few final words to carry with me into battle. Someone was bound to find them if I were wounded or killed.

Here's what I wrote.

> *To you who read these humble pages, I ask that when I quit this life, at the hour no one can evade; when the devil crowds around my deathbed and my soul leaves my body, you will come to my defense and let God know that the good in me outweighed the evil, and that my days were spent in His service, bringing faith to a fallen world.*
>
> *If I die in battle and lie unburied in the sand, please, may*

the person who finds me bring me to Rome and bury me along
the via Labicana, near the site of the two laurels, in the chapel
of my holy friends Peter and Marcellinus. If I am not found, if
no one closes my eyes and washes my wounds, and I lie in a
strange land, carrion for birds and dogs, let someone carry out
the ritual for me in Rome, though I'm far away, and honor me
with an empty tomb. Should it please God, I'll join my parents
in the life to come. Together we'll wander through sweet-smelling
laurel groves while Christ the shepherd plays His seven-stringed
lyre. When night falls, we'll sit together and partake of the holy
meal in the house of the Lord.

Early morning. Dawn on its way. I re-read my final words.
More than a bit inflated, I'd say. But what can you expect from a
Roman deacon raised in the lap of the Church?

I head downstairs with Peter in my arms, treading lightly
so Saint Sergius doesn't hear me clomping down the steps at
this ungodly hour and try to say goodbye. Romulus whinnies. I
can see the whites of his eyes. "We'll be back or we won't," I tell
him. "God knows the story. He'll let us know the ending when
he's ready."

AN AFTERWORD

◆———◆———◆

A FTER SIX WEEKS ON THE ROAD, I WAS COMING UNHINGED. TRAVEL WRITING IS AS GOOD AS IT GETS, THEY SAY, BUT THERE'S NOTHING SPECIAL about tearing around Europe, fingering sheets and towels, sticking your fat lens into other people's lives. My suite last night had its own infinity pool, and a shower with multiple showerheads, two for each orifice, but I would have chucked it all for a night in a dump with someone I cared about.

So I was thinking as I pulled into the ancient Adriatic port of Kotor, an hour or so south of Dubrovnik. With its melancholy squares and narrow, weed-choked walkways, Kotor was a town every travel writer could get off on. But I was tired of waking each morning with my toothbrush in a new glass, tired of passing through. It was time to learn how to travel without leaving home.

I was standing below the massive bell-towers of Saint Tryphon's cathedral, contemplating an uncertain future, when a powerful hand clamped down on my wrist. I whirled around. A shrunken old man smiled toothlessly up at me. Before I could pull away, he began assaulting me with his erudition.

In 890, he said, a Byzantine ship carrying relics to Venice was driven ashore at Kotor during a heavy storm. Taking this as a cue from heaven, the town purchased the skull and assorted bones of Tryphon, the patron saint of gardeners, and sanctified their new cathedral in his name. They also bought several bodies worth of votive legs and arms.

I had seen many relics in my life, but I had never thought about the people who made a living buying and selling them. Who were they, I wondered, these Road Warriors of the Dark Ages, these Willy Lomans, who worked the pilgrim routes of Europe, buying and selling body parts? Were they early sales-men, working on commission? Did they dig up the remains of Roman gladiators and fishmongers, and pass them off as saints and martyrs? Were they soldiers of God, spreading the faith?

When my father was alive and well, back in the 1980s, he traveled the roads of Europe buying and selling women's hats. I imagined him now, living in a third-floor walk-up in Rome, buying and selling human limbs—skulls, arms, torsos, toes. I saw him entertaining valued customers with mugs of honeyed wine, or sitting alone, curled over his desk, his pale but earnest face lost in shadows as he mulled over his accounts. Wooden shelves climbed the walls behind him, crowded with relics, each with its own tiny white tag: Saint Sebastian's rib (punctured), $29.95; the head of John the Baptist, marked down from $79 to $49.95.

The subject of sacred bones was delightfully disturbing to me, with just the right touch of the forbidden and the arcane. And so I returned to New York, submitted my travel manuscript, and plunged into the world of the living dead. My next assignment, a rich man's guide to Bali, wasn't due for months. Until then my life was my own.

I began my pilgrimage by reading everything I could find on daily life in early ninth-century Europe. It was a sensible place to begin. The relic trade was soaring then among the newly Christianized Franks (think France, Germany, northern Spain, and northern Italy), and no church or chapel could be sanctified without one. If you were someone like my father, hoping to turn a quick profit in an up-and-coming business, the relic market was the place to be.

Some relics were objects that came in touch with the saints and martyrs or were identified with them in some way—a drop of blood from the stigmata, a sliver of the Cross. Others were body parts—the larger and more recognizable the better. Of all the relics, none were expected to perform more spectacular miracles and attract more pilgrim silver than the earthly remains of the early Christian saints and martyrs (a saint lived for God, a martyr died for him). Some of them waited for Judgment Day in the Holy Land, others bid their time in neglected tombs outside the walls of Rome. Each winter grave diggers dug up these tombs, and each spring, as soon as the snows melted from the Alpine passes, they trudged north with their sacred baggage, visiting churches and fairs, filling orders from the previous summer and drumming up business for the year to come.

A whole new literary form developed around these holy heists, called *translations* (meaning *transferences*)—wonderful tales of plundered tombs and hair-raising adventures as the saints and martyrs traveled to their new homes, performing miracles along the way.

The authors of these *translations* were not out to tell gripping stories that made it to best-seller lists. They hoped to spread the word that Saint So-and-So was moving into a new neighborhood after a long, grueling escape, and was reopen for business at a better address. No community would deliberately part with a popular saint, so the relics in these stories were always snatched away at night against insuperable odds. The more dangerous the rescue, the more venerable the prize; the more miraculous the saint's deliverance, the more visible the hand of God. It was a good read for the Dark Ages—if you were one of the few who knew how to read.

MY PURSUIT OF *TRANSLATIONS* TOOK ME THROUGH THE fusty stacks of New York University's Loeb Library, where I pounced upon a little volume with a big name, *The History of the Translation of the Blessed Martyrs of Christ Peter and Marcellinus*. It was written around 827 AD by Einhard, Charlemagne's famed biographer, and it was translated into English by the Harvard scholar Barrett Wendell one thousand and ninety-six years later. The Harvard University Press printed five hundred copies. It was in this book that I found my subject, the man I wanted to write about, my father, myself.

His name was Deusdona—"God's gift," in Latin. In the early ninth century he roamed through Western Europe, trafficking in bones.

Einhard tells us in his *Translation* that he ran into Deusdona in Aachen, Charlemagne's former palace, and commissioned him to deliver the remains of two fourth-century Roman martyrs, Peter and Marcellinus. The two men had been beheaded for their faith, and lay, one above the other, in a chapel in the Roman catacombs—the underground city of the dead, a few miles outside the city walls.

Here's a brief translation of the opening pages of Einhard's *History of the Translation of the Blessed Martyrs of Christ Marcellinus and Peter*. I couldn't have made it up.

> *When, still at court and busy with secular matters, I used often to think in all matter of ways about the repose which I hoped some time to enjoy, I came across a little-known place, far removed from the vulgar crowd; and by the generosity of Louis, the prince, whom I then served, I became possessed of it. This place is in the German forest which lies midway between the rivers Neckar and Main, and in our times is called Odenwald by the inhabitants and their neighbors.*
>
> *When, according to my powers and means, I had built*

there not only houses and other places of permanent hab-itation but also a church of no unsuitable design for the celebration of divine service, I began to wonder in the name and honor of what saint or martyr it had best be dedicated. And when a great deal of time had passed in this wavering of mind, it happened that a certain deacon of the Roman Church, by name Deusdona, who desired to request the help of the king in some needs of his own, came to court. When he was arranging to return to Rome, he was invited by us one day, as a matter of politeness, to come, as a visitor, to our frugal dinner; and there, while talking a good deal at table, we chanced in conversation to reach a point where mention was made of the translation of the Blessed Sebastian, and of the neglected tombs of the martyrs of which there is a great abundance in Rome.

Then, the talk turning on the dedication of our new church, I began to ask him by what means I could bring it about that some bit of the true relics of the saints, who lie at rest in Rome, could be obtained by me. Here he at first hesitated a little, and answered that he did not know how this could be managed. Then, when he perceived that I was eager and anxious about the matter, he promised that he would answer my question some other day.

Afterwards, when he was invited by me again, he presently took from the folds of his garment a written note, requesting that I should read it when alone, and that I would be so good as to tell him how I liked what was there set down.

I took the note and, as he desired it, read it when alone.
The contents were as follows: He had at home a great many rel-
ics of saints, and he was willing to give them to me if helped by
what I might do for him he could get back to Rome. He under-
stood that I had two mules. If I would give him one of these, and
send with him a trusty man of my own, who could receive the
relics from him and bring them back to me, he would send them
to me at once.

The general temper of his request pleased me; and I made up
my mind to test the value of his indefinite promise without delay.
So, having given him the animal he asked for and added money
for his journey, I ordered my notary, by name Ratleig, who had
himself made a vow to visit Rome for purposes of prayer, to go
with him. So setting out from Aix-la-Chapelle [Aix]—for at
that time the Emperor was there with his court—they came to
Soissons; and there they had some talk with Hildoin, the abbot
of the monastery of Saint-Médard, who requested the body of
the blessed martyr Tibertius should come into his possession.
Charmed by these promises, the abbot sent with them a certain
priest, a crafty man by name Lehun, with orders to bring him
the body of the aforesaid martyr when received from the deacon.
The journey thus begun, the three men made their way toward
Rome as fast as they could.

In his *Translation*, Einhard dismisses Deusdona as a man
of dubious integrity. This may have been true. But it's just as
likely that Einhard cast the deacon as a villain, a foil to Peter and

Marcellinus, in order to make the martyrs' escape from Rome seem more miraculous.

Let's give the Princeton scholar Patrick Gary the final word. In *Furta Sacra* (1978, Princeton University Press) he writes:

> *The best known of the ninth-century relic merchants was Deusdona, a deacon of the Roman Church, who provided Einhard with the bodies of Saints Peter and Marcellinus. Deusdona was no occasional thief but rather the head of a large and highly organized group of relic merchants. Envious of his friend Hildoin's acquisition of the body of Saint Sebastian, and needing important relics to endow his newly founded monastery at Mulinheim, Einhard engaged Deusdona's services for the first time in 827. A contract was drawn up, and Deusdona agreed to take Einhard's notary Ratleig to Rome with him in order to procure the relics. On their way south, they stopped at Soissons, where Hildoin contracted for the remains of Saint Tibertius. Deusdona seems to have kept his part of the bargain, but Hildoin's agent attempted to cheat Einhard out of his relics by secretly stealing them from Ratleig and returning with them to the Abbey of Saint Médard at Soissons. It was only later, when by chance Einhard learned from Hildoin that Soissons had the relics of Peter and Marcellinus, that he was able to force their surrender. This attempted deceit and the subsequent pretensions of the monastery of Saint Médard to possess the relics, led Einhard to write his version of the translation. In*

*spite of the general acceptance of this account, the monastery
continued over the subsequent centuries to claim possession of
the two martyrs.*

I needed to begin research for my next book, the thoroughly
dispensable *Sybaritic Traveler's Guide to Bali: Paradise on $1,000 a
Day*. But there was something I had to do first, for myself and for
my father—and that was to visit Rome and stand before the altar
in the chapel where Peter and Marcellinus had slept together for
more than five hundred years—before their earthly remains
were stolen. If I moved quickly, I could slip in a short visit to
Einhard's church in Mulinheim (Seliginstadt, Germany, today)
on my way home, and pay homage to the two martyrs. If they
were still there.

If they had ever been there.

The chapel of Peter and Marcellinus was closed to the public,
as I feared, but a friend of a friend worked for the Italian Mission
to the U.N. in New York, and weaseled an official pass for me
through the Commissionaire Pontifico Archeologie Christiana,
on via Napoleone.

I arrived in the Eternal City at dawn, feeling, as I do after
all overnight flights, like a newborn cat waiting to be licked off. I
grabbed the bus into town and left my bag at the first hotel I could
find—a dark, cramped *pensione* across from the train station—the
sort of hellhole guidebooks describe as colorful or softened with
age. I arrived at the office of the *commissionaire* as the doors were
opening. A tall, thin man in long-tasseled loafers ushered me into

his office. He was expecting me, he said. Some spittle bubbled in a corner of his mouth while he talked; his tongue darted out and licked it away, leaving a shiny film.

"Give this to the caretaker tomorrow at ten," he said, scribbling a few words on a yellow sticky note. "He won't be happy if you're late."

The next morning I hopped into a cab and rode two miles down the via Casilina to the chapel of Peter and Marcellinus. What in the ninth century must have been a dreary, rural landscape infested with weeds is today an industrial suburb infested with body repair shops, ferro-concete housing blocks, and discount clothing stores with names like Play Back. Shirtless men disappeared under the hoods of battered cars. A woman stood in an asphalt parking lot, watering a tire filled with purple peonies.

The caretaker, a squat, balding man, was waiting for me at the catacomb gate. It squeaked open, as old gates do. The stone steps leading down into the chapel—perhaps the same ones Deusdona stumbled on more than a thousand years before— were blocked by a rusty grate, so we entered through the small, charmless chapel of Tibertius, which belongs today to a school for nuns.

Swinging his Coleman lantern like a censor, the caretaker led me through a labyrinth of dark, narrow passageways. The dampness was oppressive. My bones ached. Water dripped from roots reaching down from the ceiling, just as Deusdona said they did. Robbers had done their damage over the years, and most of the graves were nothing but dark, open pits, one above the other, like empty berths on a Pullman train.

The caretaker spoke only Italian. I spoke only English. It was not a relationship made in heaven. But I knew exactly what he meant when he screamed at me for trying to take pictures. This was a sacred place still.

The chapel was not much to see. The altar was gone. So was the marble floor. All I could make out were some smashed marble pillars, and a mound of earth with two gashes, where Peter and Marcellinus once lay, one above the other.

The caretaker waved. It was time to leave. I tipped him. He smiled and shook my hand as though we were old friends.

TO REACH EINHARD'S CHURCH IN MULINHEIM I TOOK AN afternoon train to Milan, and then an overnight sleeper to Frankfurt. There's nothing I love more than sleeping on a train—locking myself in a private compartment, crawling between the cold, crisp sheets, raising the thick, heavy shades and staring out at the solitary farmhouse lights and at the stationmasters waving their lanterns on empty platforms, telling us it's okay to carry on.

There had been a slipup, though. I was in a compartment for two. It was almost midnight when I boarded, and the man in the lower berth was snoring. I flipped on the lights briefly and his eyes opened and shut. I stripped down to my underwear and climbed into the upper. Having no window, I fell quickly into a dreamless sleep.

When I woke up it was early morning and we were already in Frankfurt. My roommate was dressed and sitting on his bed, nursing a coffee. *"Guten morgen,"* I said.

He asked me in English what had brought me to Italy, and I told him about my search for Peter and Marcellinus. He stared at me for a long time. "I'm a university professor," he said. "Peter and Marcellinus are my specialty. I was just in Rome, visiting their tomb."

We met each other's glances in silence. "Perhaps they wanted us to get together," I smiled. "I wonder what they had in mind."

I asked him to draw me a picture of the tomb as it looked in the ninth century, but the conductor came rushing through the car, telling everyone to hurry off, so we grabbed our bags and went our separate ways. He was lost in the crowds before I realized that we had never introduced ourselves. I had never even asked for his card.

An expensive cab ride later, I was standing alone in the abbey church in Seliginstadt, starring at the silver reliquary that is still believed to hold the remains of Peter and Marcellinus. Whether it does or not, I have no idea. Nor does anyone else. Deusdona would have said it doesn't matter whether these are sacred bones or not, so long as we believe in them. I give him the final word.

I took a few pictures from different angles, with a range of exposures. I was restless and vaguely disappointed. I had expected the saints to blind me with their celestial light, but all I saw was a silver box below an altar in a dignified old church. I RUSHED TO FRANKFURT AND CAUGHT AN AFTERNOON flight to New York. I was strapped in and waiting for the runway to clear when I made up my mind to cancel my trip to Bali—I knew a thousand travel writers who would sell their mothers to take my place—and try to write my own account of Deusdona's life. It would be based on Einhard's *Translation* and on all I had read and absorbed about life in Europe in the early Middle Ages. I would be playing blindman's buff with the truth, but I might end up learning how to travel without leaving home.

I found a laundry receipt in my wallet and scribbled on the back,

Deusdona is the name I go by. God's gift. I'd prefer the name of a Roman senator, but you can't improve on Deusdona, not if you make a living buying and selling sacred bones.

It wasn't a bad beginning.

Suddenly the engines roared and the plane lurched forward. I gripped the armrests nervously and told myself it was just a matter of time before we were above the clouds.

ACKNOWLEDGMENTS

MANY THANKS TO ART DIRECTOR DOMINI DRAGOONE FOR HER COMPELLING SENSE OF DESIGN, AND TO LEAH GORDON, MANaging editor of Four Winds Press, for shepherding the book through every stage of production. It was a treat working with such pros.

Thanks, too, to Kelly Regan for her invaluable advice; to my son Evan Spring, who helped edit the original manuscript and gave me support when I most needed it; to my agent Kevin Mulroy; and to my publisher Bill Newlin, who shares my love for bones.

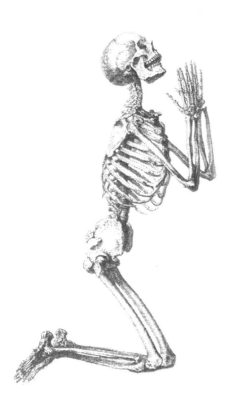

ABOUT THE AUTHOR

◆——————◆——————◆

MIKE SPRING WAS BORN IN NEW YORK CITY IN 1941. HE HAS DEGREES IN ENGLISH LITERATURE FROM HAVERFORD COLLEGE and Columbia University. After his junior year in college he spent ten months hitching around the world.

On his return, he worked for more than two decades as editorial director of Fodor's Travel Guides and publisher and vice-president of Frommer's Travel Guides. He and his wife Janis have written three books—*After the Affair* (HarperCollins), *How Can I Forgive You?* (Harper Collins) and *Life with Pop: Lessons on Caring for an Aging Parent* (Penguin). They live in Westport, Connecticut. Between them, they have four sons, Declan and Evan Spring, and Aaron and Max Abrahms.

ALSO AVAILABLE FROM FOUR WINDS PRESS

The Ambassador to Brazil by Peter Hornbostel. $15.95, 978-1-940423-11-1. Anthony Carter is the United States ambassador to Brazil in March 1964, when a secret task force of U.S. warships sets sail to help the military in a planned coup d'état. Hornbostel weaves fact and fiction to tell a tale of political intrigue, a love affair with a Brazilian mistress, Marina, and Carter's struggle between the deceptions that surround his public work and the intensity of his private life.

Apples & Oranges: In Praise of Comparisons by Maarten Asscher. $15.95, 978-1-940423-06-7. Are comparisons across genres inherently invalid, or can they be illuminating? In 22 wide-ranging essays, Dutch author Maarten Asscher maintains that comparisons can be the highest form of argument.

17 Stone Angels: A Novel by Stuart Archer Cohen. $15.95, 978-1-940423-05-0. Crimes of the lowest and highest order come together in Buenos Aires, one of the most dangerous and beautiful cities on earth, when corrupt police chief Miguel Fortunato is assigned to invesitgate a murder he committed.

The Voyage of the UnderGod: A Comedy by Kirby Smith. $14.95, 978-1-940423-02-9. A political satire about charismatic right-winger Luther Dorsey's last grasp for the greatness he thinks he deserves, *UnderGod* tells the tale of a reality-TV tall ship's sailing voyage around Cape Horn.

Laughing Cult: Poems by Kevin McCaffrey. $13.95, 978-1-940423-00-5. A highly accessible collection that combines a quirky sensibility with traditional poetic forms to create miniature sketches marked by romantic ambiguity, occultism, science fiction, and quirky angst.

Invisible World by Stuart Archer Cohen. $15.95, 978-1-940423-04-3. An invitation from a dead man propels Chicagoan Andrew Mann to abandon his mundane existence and embark on a perilous journey from Hong Kong to Inner Mongolia in search of a fabled map of the *Invisible World*.

CPSIA information can be obtained at www.ICGtesting.com
Printed in the USA
LVOW11s1132070515

437582LV00002B/2/P